LAURA

DARK
Karma

SWORD OF
VENGEANCE

outskirts
press

Author Notes

I want to extend a heartfelt thank you to my beta readers, Kay McB and Denise O'Donnell. Your helpful suggestions uncovered character inconsistencies, plot holes, and the wrong forms of to, too, week, weak, peal, peel, among other things! The fact that both of you enjoyed this story, even with all of the needed corrections, really boosts my confidence to continue writing. To my characters, thank you for living inside my head and my heart, and pushing me to tell your stories. I couldn't do it without you and the surprising plot twists you give me. To my dear readers, thank you for taking the time to read *Dark Karma: Sword of Vengeance*. I sincerely hope that you like it, and look forward to the next one.

CHAPTER 1

Love Her Madly

Sharing a lusty kiss, Luke and Nina moved into the bedroom. Clothes were shed in less than a minute and they fell into bed, making love like starving savages. After the rapture, he looked into her eyes and said, "I love you, Nina." From the shocked expression on her face, he thought she was going to push him away and tell him to leave. Her mouth was slightly agape, her beautiful eyes wide and questioning, and she said nothing. He couldn't believe he had blurted out his feelings for her. He had never said those three little words to any woman. And yet, he meant them. Their bodies remained joined together and she continued gazing into his dark eyes, a thousand questions running through her mind.

She was astounded and speechless. She wasn't expecting a declaration of love from the worldly, handsome, and muscular Luke Decker, her longtime friend with benefits. He said he wanted to live with her to keep her safe from the thugs out to get her, but *love*? Luke had never been in a serious relationship in his thirty-nine years of life. She didn't think he was the type of man who would commit to a woman, and she was a free spirit who kept telling herself that men were just for fun. She was fearful of getting her heart broken again.

Finally recovering her voice, she smiled and playfully rubbed his shaved head replying, "When did this happen?"

Even though he wasn't expecting her to say it back, he was hoping for something other than her question and was relieved that she hadn't kicked him out of her bed. He couldn't stand the thought of her with other men, not anymore. She had been on his mind for months before he came to visit, and Cupid's arrow struck him hard when he laid eyes on her after eight months apart. His urge to love and protect her was overwhelming, and no other woman had ever made him feel this way. He knew deep in his soul that she was the one, and if he didn't speak up now there was a chance he might lose her to Elliott Greenwood. He didn't like that guy. His instincts told him Elliott was dangerous, despite his gentlemanly demeanor. He could spot the type instantly, like when mild-mannered Mike Collins turned out to be a deranged serial killer and abducted his brother's lady love, Amber. Once, Mike had been good friends with his brother Bryce, and there was something about Mike that Luke had never liked.

Returning her smile, he answered, "You've been on my mind for months, and when I came to visit and saw you sweeping the barn, it hit me hard and I realized you were the one. I didn't want to admit it to myself, and I'll be honest, learning about your friendship with Elliott makes me jealous. I felt it as soon as I saw the picture of the two of you on your wall. Yes, I want to live with you to protect you, but it's more than that. You are the total package. You're beautiful, smart, strong, sexy, talented, and the perfect woman for me. I promise I won't try to change you. I love you just the way you are. You can tell me to get lost whenever you want.

"Bryce wants to expand Decker Martial Arts outside of the D.C. area, and this would be a great town to open a new studio. Teaching martial arts will be a wonderful change for me, and I know he will give me free reign to get that started here. I'm no longer working for the CIA. I quit three weeks ago. I'm not even a consultant. I'm fully retired and my globetrotting days are done."

She gasped in surprise, her eyes widening once again, "I thought you would be an operative for life! I'm happy to hear that you want to settle down, but I'm wondering ... you've been free and single your whole life. Maybe you only think that you *love* me because there's another man interested. If I give my heart to you, will you be faithful?" she asked, thinking it was best to find this out up front. She wouldn't settle for anything less if she was going to take the fall again.

He continued looking into her lovely, hazel brown eyes framed with long, dark eyelashes. The ring around her iris was brown, and the centers were lighter brown with hints of gold. He answered in a serious tone, "Yes, I will be faithful, and I don't make promises lightly. I rarely make them at all. And it's not just because Elliott's in the picture. I know you can have your choice of men, and it never bothered me before. But now it does. You don't have to decide right now about living together, but I need to know if you'll give us a chance. I'm ready to move down here and can get my own place if you need more time."

She was thinking of how she would break the news to Elliott, knowing that he was secretly in love with her. She was attracted to him and he was a good friend. Although when she fantasized about taking their friendship to the next level, it left her with a sick feeling in the pit of her stomach. She knew Elliott was hiding something, and despite Luke's non-committal track record, he had always been honest with her. She had worked hard over the past three years to keep her feelings for Luke under control. Their one night stand three years ago evolved into a friends-with-benefits relationship, and she had struggled to keep from falling in love with him. Perhaps it was safe to do so now. She was unaware that Luke had fought his own strong feelings for her too.

They had worked together for many years, and were close friends. Nina had been despondent over a broken engagement. She had caught her fiancé Jerry in bed with two women a few days before their wedding. Luke had offered her a shoulder to cry on, and it had led to something more. He was happy to provide rebound sex whenever she wanted with no strings for either of them. It suited them both, even though she wished for more from him. She didn't have any trouble attracting men, however she usually fell for the wrong type. Her current unencumbered life of casual sex with handsome men helped to insulate her from falling hard for just one man. Being gifted in the psychic arts, she knew how to project a femme fatale vibe that sent men swarming to her like flies. This enabled her to talk herself out of falling in love by regularly enjoying other fish in the sea. She had rules, though: she never seduced a man who had a wife or girlfriend, and required her lovers to use protection. She never forgot to take her birth control pills either.

She wasn't getting any younger, her thirty-eighth birthday was three months away, so maybe it was time to let go of her fears and take a chance on love again. She might have been mistaken thinking Luke would be a guaranteed heartbreak, and there was only one way to find out.

She kissed him and said, "I want to give us a try. I'd prefer that you move down here and get your own place. This way we can test the waters without jumping in head first."

"Are you sure?"

"Yes."

"You won't regret it. I'm looking forward to pleasing you. Not just sexually, but in all ways," he promised.

Despite his words, they spent the rest of the day and into the evening making love over and over again, both of them growing more voracious with each tryst. Finally sated, they fell asleep at 8:30 p.m. and didn't wake up until early the next morning when they heard her rooster, Rogue crowing.

She awoke in his arms and softly said, "Rogue does this every morning."

He hugged her closer in his heavily muscled arms and replied with a laugh, "No problem. He let me sleep in this morning. I'm usually up before now."

"It's a good thing we're both early birds," she remarked. "I want coffee, what about you?"

"Actually, I'm thinking of something else," he replied gliding his hands over her hips and pressing her against his erection.

Without saying a word, she climbed on top of him and they slowly rocked together to paradise.

"What have you done to me, love?" he asked when she collapsed on top of him and kissed his neck. "I can't get enough of you. I could live like this forever, with you on top of me."

Laughing, she kissed him and rolled out of his arms. Getting out of bed she felt the need to stretch. He lingered in bed watching her stand and stretch her arms up high, thinking she was the most incredible woman in the world. He admired her lithe, athletic body. She was slim, barely five feet three inches and perfectly proportioned. She wore her dark brown hair short and pixie-like, but not close-cropped. She was an adventurous tomboy at heart, and he loved that about her.

"Nina Perotti, you're my sexy little fairy goddess," he said, appreciating her figure. One thing which perplexed him though was how she healed so fast after suffering a gunshot wound to her leg. She walked with a slight limp and he could see bruising, but her recovery was miraculous. Granted she got lucky and the bullet didn't do major damage, yet he still had questions he would ask her later.

Her eyes sparkled and she replied, "And I can create magic too."

She was an astral traveler and clairvoyant working as a consultant to the CIA. Skilled in the art of manipulating energy, she had tapped into the strong feelings they had for each other and energetically magnified them into an all-consuming hunger. She silently rejoiced in her feelings for him, reciprocated at last.

"I'm a prime example of your handiwork, sweetheart," he replied, winking.

He was planning to drive home to Vienna, Virginia, that day, and had stayed in a hotel the previous night. Nina and Luke had helped Bryce rescue Amber from the clutches of a psychotic madman. Nina used her gift of telekinesis to keep Mike from raping and killing Amber, while Bryce used his talent for astral travel to find out where Mike lived and raced down to Georgia to rescue her. Fearing for his brother's life, Luke followed him after enlisting Nina's help. Amber was in the hospital now with Bryce by her side. She was recovering after nearly dying from smoke inhalation when Mike set his house on fire and left her tied up in his basement. Unfortunately, Mike had escaped.

Since Nina agreed to a relationship with Luke, he wasn't anxious to leave. She lived alone in a rural area near Charlottesville, Virginia, on a small farm with a few goats, some chickens, a cat, and a horse. The rolling hills and peaceful countryside were a slice of heaven. When she wasn't working on a project with the CIA, she spent her days doing yoga at sunrise, tending to her garden and farm animals, making soap to sell at farmer's markets along with produce from her large vegetable garden, riding her horse around her five acres of land, and writing songs.

Her house was vandalized while she helped Amber, and the front door and several windows were boarded shut. They had spent the night in her house, using the back entrance after getting her place cleaned up and seeing to her animals. She was staying with Elliott until she could get her house repaired and new security system installed. Luke didn't want her returning to Elliott's house and wanted to know what the thugs were after. He broached the subject as soon as they finished eating breakfast.

"You know I was planning to head back today, but since you agreed to be my love I have no reason to rush home. I would like to stay here instead. I'll provide the extra protection until you get your new doors, windows, and security system. Once everything is installed, I'll head back to Vienna, pack up my stuff and move down here. I'll start looking for a rental today," he said. "So, I *must* know what they were looking for. I don't want any secrets between us. They put a bullet in your leg, hit you on the head with the butt of a pistol and left you here to die. You were in a coma! Thank God the police found you in time and called an ambulance. And, how did you bounce back from that gunshot wound so quickly?"

"Do you remember the child slavery ring I helped bust?" she asked.

"Yeah, that was about four years ago, right? I wish I had worked on that one," he replied.

"Those criminals were the scum of the earth posing as benevolent humanitarians while masterminding a child slavery ring, leading many unfortunate little ones to a life of misery and ruin. After the fight was over and the bad guys hauled away in handcuffs, I surveyed the ransacked office from the astral realm ... and it called to me," she said.

She had played a crucial role in helping the CIA, FBI, and Interpol locate and bring them to justice. Being a CIA psychic for over fifteen years, her ability to uncover hidden information and physical items was unparalleled. Her skills included telekinesis on both the physical and astral planes, with the unique talent of bringing objects back with her.

"Did you take something from the astral?" he asked.

Nodding she replied, "Yes, but it's not something I normally do. Taking items while in astral form always makes me violently sick when I return to my body. I figure it's the universe's way of punishing me for stealing, but I couldn't help myself."

"Tell me more, my sweet," he said, reaching out to hold her hand.

"The room began to fill with twinkling, dust-like particles, which were coming from behind an overturned desk. I looked behind it and saw a softly glowing rock. It looked like a common river rock, but it was emitting a warm, golden glow. Its twinkling dust surrounded me, begging me to take it. My astral body was disguised as a Pitbull. It's safer for me to shift into an animal in case malevolent entities are lurking about. At that moment I didn't care if it made me sick when I returned. I was taking this rock home. When I returned here, I expected to be running to the bathroom and puking my guts out which would be followed by a migraine. The sickness never came," she stated. "I carry it with me sometimes, although it's so powerful it takes time to get adjusted to the energy."

"When you got home, did you have the rock in your mouth? How do you bring items back?" he asked with a chuckle, amazed that she could shapeshift on the astral.

She laughed and said, "Yes, I had it in my mouth. How else would a dog carry something? First, I concentrate on the object and there will be a moment when I can touch it. Then I get a tingling sensation in my hands and fingers. Once I grab hold of it, it stays with me unless I change my mind and set it back down."

"Since you were disguised as a dog, did you get the sensation in your paws?"

"Yes."

"Does this unusual rock enhance your abilities?"

"Yes. I'm glad you have an open mind about these things; otherwise, you will freak out when I tell you that it enables me to teleport wherever I wish to go. I focus on my destination, relax, close my eyes and I'm there. I've only done it a few times. It will sometimes create things from my thoughts, so I have to be very careful when I handle it. I keep it hidden most of the time. I should have been more cautious when I first started working with it by building psychic walls to block other astral travelers. I failed to do that, and now someone knows I have it and will go to great lengths to take it. I don't blame them for wanting it, but it's mine. In answer to your earlier question, I used the rock to help heal my leg. Obviously, it's not one-hundred percent better, but it's pretty close. I didn't want the doctors asking too many questions, so I didn't heal it completely. I'm going to let it finish healing on its own," she concluded.

He was astonished and thought this was the stuff of fantasy. Gently rubbing his thumb over hers, he asked, "Where did you teleport to? And what have you created with it?"

Amused, she replied, "I was thinking about my sister, Madison, and how I hadn't visited her for almost a year. The next thing I know, I'm standing in her living room and she sees me and screams. I was standing there with my mouth open and unable to speak. We gradually recovered from the shock, and now whenever I talk to her she asks me about my adventures with it."

"Wow … I guess everything we think of as being just a fantasy, is actually real," he replied. "Did you think yourself home?"

She laughed, answering, "That's exactly what I did. I'm glad she lives alone so we didn't have to explain it to anyone."

"Tell me what you created!" he insisted.

"I created wealth. I'm rich beyond my wildest dreams, but I prefer to live simply and work now and then for the Agency. I don't want unnecessary attention. Would you like to see how it works?"

"Yes!"

She closed her eyes for a second, taking a deep breath. Then he watched her lift her hand and draw a square shape into the air with her index finger. She reached inside retrieving a small wooden box and setting it on the table.

"You look like you've just seen a ghost," she said while he sat there with his mouth open; his dark brown eyes wide with disbelief.

"You are truly gifted," he commented, his heart thumping. He had seen many extraordinary things in his life, but nothing like this.

She opened the box to display a plain looking, smooth, grayish-white rock which fit neatly in her hand.

"Plain and powerful," he said. "Can you retrieve it from anywhere?"

"Yes, that's what I did in the hospital. It's not completely plain though. Look at the carving on this side," she said, turning it over and showing him the etching of a large tree carved into the stone. "It must have been spelled by a powerful psychic or shaman. I get the feeling that it hasn't revealed all of its secrets to me yet."

"Can I hold it?" he asked.

"Sure. Place it in your palm and think of something you'd like to buy me," she joked.

He held it in his palm, closing his fingers around it. He felt a pleasing surge of warmth encompass his body. Its energy made him feel happy and hopeful, almost giddy. His expression softened, he looked into her eyes and thought of something he'd like to buy her one day. He saw it in a magazine advertisement recently and admired its simple beauty. To his amazement, it materialized on the table.

She opened the small velvet box that appeared in front of her, and squealed with delight. "Oh my God! Luke!"

He was so shocked that the color drained from his face and he set the magic rock back in its wooden box. He blamed it on the intense happiness he felt when holding it, and the surprising mental picture of Nina wearing a long white dress entered his mind. He didn't think it would actually appear, nor did he want her to know he was planning their future together. He was concerned that she would think he was moving too fast.

"N-N-Nina ... I was h-h-hoping, s-s-s-someday ..." He stopped talking, embarrassed by the stuttering. This hadn't happened to him since he was in elementary school. Often teased by the other children, his parents enrolled him in speech class and he worked diligently to correct his impediment. He vowed to become big, strong, and fearsome when he grew up and was the type of person who accomplished every goal he set for himself. None of the dangerous, death-defying missions he went on, both as a Navy SEAL and CIA operative, had ever caused him to stutter when he spoke. She was turning his world upside down.

She gazed at him with love and kindness. "It's breathtaking. Maybe one day we will take that leap. Is it okay if I try it on, and then we can send it back?"

He breathed a sigh of relief as the anxiety left his body. "Yes, please do."

She slipped the sparkling diamond ring onto her left ring finger, and laid her hand on the table.

"It looks good on you," he said, taking her left hand and kissing it. "You don't have to send it back. It can be a promise ring. If you'd like a different style, I want to know."

"It's perfect, and I love it because you thought of it. I have an idea. There's room in the box for this and we can keep them stored together. It will be there if and when the time comes," she replied.

"I agree. Although, you can wear it anytime," he said, grinning and pleased that she wasn't upset with him.

She returned his smile, slipping the diamond ring off her finger and putting it back in the little velvet box. She placed the box in the wooden one next to the rock and closed it. Drawing the square in the air once again, she slid the wooden box back into its hiding place.

"Now I've seen everything. Nothing will *ever* surprise me again," he said with a chuckle.

She got up from the table and came over to him. Pulling her onto his lap he kissed her senseless.

"I want you again," she whispered. "Right here, right now."

"Then, you shall have me," he answered. "Straddle me like you did when we woke up. These chairs are sturdy."

She did as he asked, slipping off her robe and mounting him.

"Come with me, my naughty Nina."

"I will, over and over, my lusty Luke."

It didn't take long for them to find paradise for the second time that morning.

After taking a long shower together, they got dressed and walked outside to take care of the animals. The first stop was her barn to feed the chickens and goats, and then the stable to take a ride on her horse, Buttercup. Luke sat behind her, his arms firmly around her waist and loving the feel of having her body in constant contact with his. She relaxed against him while they rode around her five acres of property. She knew it was time to have another discussion.

"I think Elliott's going to be disappointed when I tell him about us. He will probably want to remain friends though, and I hate to cut him out of my life completely. What kind of boundaries do you want to set with regard to friends of the opposite sex?" she asked remembering how Jerry betrayed her trust.

Luke was quiet for a few moments collecting his thoughts ... *I want her to stay away from him* ... "This is new territory for me. I don't have a problem with you being friends with a man — or Elliott. I do have a problem with you going out alone with one of them. If you want to meet somewhere for a casual lunch, that's fine. If you want to chat on the phone or text now and then, I'm okay with that too. I'm fine with any of your friends, male or female, coming over and joining us for dinner or going out with us. And I want you to know that you are the only female friend I've enjoyed benefits with. You can rest assured that the most I would do is talk on the phone with a female friend, or maybe meet her for lunch. And you would know the place and time and would be invited too. I don't want you worrying about those things. I'm nothing like Jerry. You are my first priority and my *only* woman."

"That's good to know. I think I'll call Elliott after we finish our ride and let him know about our change in status," she said. "I can get my things from his house later."

Leaning down he kissed her cheek and said, "That's a good idea. Maybe he'll bring them by and you won't have to go get them. I think we're a perfect fit. My parents had a close, loving marriage until Mom died in a car accident. Her death broke my father's heart, and he died about two years later from terminal cancer; he just gave up on life. Both of their deaths had a profound effect on me and I decided that I never wanted to love someone like that because it would hurt too much if I lost her.

"That's the main reason I've never had a long-term romantic relationship with anyone; that and my line of work. However, I want more out of life, including a special woman to love and take care of, and a normal job where I don't have to constantly travel. Although, I would travel anywhere with you."

"You know, the reason I've been a man-eater since my break-up with Jerry is that I didn't want to get hurt again. I've been fighting my feelings for you since we started having *benefits*. Being with other men was the only way I could keep from falling for you. I've had feelings for Elliott now and then, but something's off with him. I never pursued anything more with him for that reason. I didn't bother to investigate what it might be because I respected our friendship. Now that I know you want a future with me, I want it too," she said.

"I'm crazy about you Nina, and I'm never letting you go. I've been fighting my feelings for you too. I wanted to make you mine, but I was afraid of commitment and you weren't ready for another relationship. I had to mature a bit more. You've been on my mind for months and I was planning to come and see you even before I asked for your help in saving Amber. On another subject, I think you should use your special talents to find out who's after your rock."

"I'm planning to astral travel soon and see what I can uncover," she replied.

"I know Bryce would like to help you. He's grateful for you help-ing Amber and tormenting Mike," Luke stated.

"I can still torment Mike while he's on the run."

"As long as you come back safe and sound, and share your stories with me in the morning," he said.

"I will," she replied with a contented sigh.

Elliott knew Luke was going to be a thorn in his side when it came to Nina. He met the man when he stopped by to pick up Nina yesterday and didn't like that he was tough competition with his body-builder physique. Elliott spent the morning straightening up his garage and dwelling on the fact that Luke and Nina spent the night together, undoubtedly enjoying hot and heavy lovemaking, and he was growing angrier by the hour. Elliott and Nina had spent a wonderful evening together the other night talking, and watching funny movies, and now this guy ruins everything. He cursed himself for falling in love with the woman he was supposed to befriend just to steal the rock. Elliott was a professional thief and people paid him top dollar to steal pre-cious items. He used his astral abilities to track down the items people wanted, and then devised a plan and stole them. His father had been a greedy, talented crook who taught him the tricks of the trade. He felt it was important to project an impeccable, nice-guy image so no one would ever suspect he led a double life. Knowing how much Elliott loved the ocean, he encouraged him to join the Navy which helped his son maintain an all-American good-guy charade.

Elliott's mother died in childbirth and he grew up among his father's never-ending supply of lady friends, as he was an incurable womanizer. Elliott admired his father and wanted to be just like him with regards to taking what he wanted regardless if it belonged to someone else. He wasn't a womanizer though. Being raised without a strong maternal figure, when he fell for someone he didn't want to lose them and became possessive and domineering. This led to a lifetime of women leaving him for that reason.

He was a handsome man, standing six feet tall with thick, salt and pepper hair and brown eyes. At fifty years old, he was in good physical shape and still turned ladies' heads. The plan was to gain Nina's trust, become her confidant and get her to reveal her secrets. He knew she was a free spirit and never planned to pursue anything other than friendship because he would become overbearing and scare her away, like all the others. He had given up on women years ago after his wife Carol left him for doing just that. It didn't help that he physically abused her when he got angry, something he watched his father do on numerous occasions to certain women. She snuck out one day while he was at work. He came home that evening to an empty house and divorce papers on the coffee table. She took just her personal items and clothes and he never saw her again. All communication was done through her lawyer. He found out later that she ran off with another man and was living in Denmark. Fortunately, there were no children and he didn't have to endure a custody battle.

He had one other serious relationship after Carol and she left him too. He wasn't physically abusive to her, but he was so possessive that he pushed her away. In spite of his past, he was ready to try once more as a changed man and decided to make a play for Nina. He would have to do it soon before Luke beat him to it. The way Luke looked at Nina spoke volumes, and Elliott could sense there was more to Luke's feelings for her than a casual, physical relationship. His heart skipped a beat when his phone rang and he saw that it was her.

"Hello," he answered trying to sound cheery.

"Hi. I wanted to let you know that Luke is going to stay with me until I get my new security doors and windows installed," she said.

"Oh, how long will that be?" he asked disappointed that she wouldn't be returning to his house tonight.

"The new doors and windows will be installed the day after to-morrow and the security system the following day. Then he's moving down here."

"Is he moving in with you?" he asked hoping otherwise.

"No. He's going to rent a place and … date me," she replied. "Thank you for letting me stay with you. You're a great friend and I really appreciate it."

"You're welcome. When you say he's going to date you, does that mean your relationship is exclusive?"

"Yes. No more friends with benefits," she replied.

Dammit! Now I have to work even harder to win her … "Are you coming by to get your stuff?"

"Not today, but I will soon."

"Is he planning to get a job or is he independently wealthy?" he asked hoping that Luke was a no-good bum.

"He's going to open a martial arts studio. His brother owns the Decker Martial Arts Company and he'll open a branch here," she replied, sounding too cheerful for his sour mood.

"Okay. Well, give me a call when you plan to stop by," he said.

"I will. Talk to you later."

"Bye," he said, ending the call and releasing a heavy sigh. *At least he's not moving in with her. I can still see her when he's not around.* He regretted having to break into her house and physically harm her, yet would do whatever was necessary to get what he wanted. He was shocked to discover that she was telekinetic and would thwart his plan. He was certain that she had other unusual abilities and it troubled him. How else could she bounce back from a gunshot wound like it was nothing? The doctors at the hospital were dumbfounded. He wondered what else she was capable of, and how long before she learned that he was the one who broke into her home and left her for dead.

When they burst into her house terrifying her half to death, objects went flying, and he almost called off the robbery. A sharp knife flew through the air and landed in Tommy's stomach, killing him quickly as he bled out on her sunroom floor. A piece of flying glass from a broken vase stabbed Elliott's upper arm and hurt like hell. He was glad they were clad in black from head to toe and she couldn't recognize him. Burt ran after her and it was too late to turn back. Burt wanted to kill her and Elliott had to shoot her in the leg and knock her unconscious to maintain his tough guy image until he could get the information from her. He was forced to speak before he knocked her out, and disguised his voice. The sound of police sirens interrupted their plans and they ran off, leaving her lying unconscious on the floor.

He was also an experienced astral traveler. He wasn't psychic, although he could create servitors to do his bidding and view the past. Once he obtained the rock, he would be rich and powerful. He was already wealthy, and it wasn't enough for him.

The rock Nina owned was highly sought after, and he wanted it. A few fellow thieves thought it was just a legend, and weren't interested in chasing after something that didn't exist. Elliott didn't believe it existed either, until the day he stole an old Scottish sword for a client. The sword was spelled with dark magic for use against enemies. He'd felt a connection with it as soon as he touched it, and decided, then and there, that it would be his. He had told his client that he was unable to obtain the sword, and refunded his money. The sword looked ancient, its true age unknown, and he had enjoyed staring at the dark red stone in its hilt. He had attempted to view the sword's history, but was blocked each time he tried. He had found that when he held the sword and asked questions, he was rewarded with the answers he needed in the form of mental images. He had asked about the lucky rock and was led to Nina's location.

When he had first started watching her from the astral realm, he hadn't seen anything unusual; just a pretty woman going about her everyday life. He became frustrated and decided to look at her past to find out when she began using it. He'd watched her manifest stacks of cash and increase her bank balance electronically while holding the rock, and wasted no time in moving to Charlottesville and winning her friendship. He had bought a secluded ranch and joined the same rural co-op as she. The co-op was made up of property owners who looked after each other's animals and estates when they were out of town. They held frequent social gatherings and went on excursions.

Further enhancing his cover, he'd taken a job as a swimming instructor. He was a retired Navy diver and an expert swimmer. He had continued spying on her from the astral plane, yet was unable to find the rock's hiding place. He didn't know that she was also an astral traveler. She knew how to cloak herself and hide her identity by creating a mirage around her house to block those on the astral plane who might be passing through. The mirage showed nothing more than her quiet country home and her playing the guitar, singing, watching TV, and other ordinary things.

He would spend the rest of his day planning and scheming how to win Nina's affection and ultimately, claim her rock.

"So, do you think he was upset with your news?" Luke asked.

"Yes. He sounded distant, but I'm not going to worry about it," she replied.

"Would you like to go with me to check out an apartment?" he asked.

"Sure. Where is it?

"According to Google Maps, its eight miles from here, in a development called Pine Ridge Commons," he replied.

"I know that area. Those are luxury apartments and there's a large strip mall two miles south of there. You might find an available storefront for your studio too," she said.

"Let's go, love," he said, taking her hand and walking out the back door.

The two-bedroom two-bath apartment was available for rent immediately, and he signed a six-month lease hoping that she would be ready to live together by then.

"This is nice," she said, appreciating the light and airy space with hardwood floors, an open kitchen, long balcony, and spacious bedrooms with walk-in closets.

"It was the closest one I could find," he said, placing the spare key and security card in her hand. "I know I have to earn your trust and by having this key, you can come over anytime day or night, and not find me with another woman."

After putting the keys into her coat pocket, she smiled and kissed him. "Thank you." Opening the sliding glass door, they stepped onto the balcony to admire the mountain view. It was a chilly and crisp November day and the sun was bright. She hadn't told him that Jerry used to live in this same building. Luke stood next to her and they gazed at the mountains in the distance …

Figuring that he would probably be sick with a hangover from his bachelor party last night, Nina wanted to surprise Jerry by going to his apartment the next morning and making him breakfast. Thinking happy thoughts of their upcoming wedding three days hence, she unlocked his door, set a bag of groceries on the kitchen counter, and walked into his bedroom. She was shocked to find him asleep in bed with two naked women wrapped around him and a pile of clothes on the floor. One of the women had her hand around his erect penis. Jerry Barlow was an attractive man of medium height and athletic build with thick brown hair and blue eyes. He made his living as a construction foreman. For a few moments all she could do was stand and stare in disbelief, her heart pounding, and then she let him have it.

"YOU FUCKING ASSHOLE! WHY, JERRY? WHY DID YOU DO

THIS?" she screamed and the picture above his bed fell off the wall, hitting him and his two women before flipping over and landing at the foot of the bed.

"Nina! Oh my God, I'm sorry honey!" he pleaded with a pounding head as the two women quickly jumped out of bed and ran from the room. Nina picked up the pile of clothes and shoes and threw them into the living room. "GET OUT OF HERE SLUTS, BEFORE I KNOCK YOUR TEETH IN!" she yelled as they hastily got dressed and ran from the apartment.

Jerry was stunned, terrified, and naked. He knew the damage she could do and he begged his case, "I promise I'll never do that again. It was one last night of fun, I swear it meant nothing to me, and I used protection! I love you, Nina. I want to spend the rest of my life with you. Please believe me."

She stood glaring at him cold and hard, simmering with anger and then she spoke: "Bullshit! If I hadn't shown up, you would have banged them again this morning, and don't you deny it! Why? Is this how our marriage will be? You cheating on me every chance you get? If you wanted to do THAT, then why did you ask me to marry you?"

"Because you are my rock and my strength and I love you. I've never cheated on you, Nina. This was a one-time fling and it will NEVER happen again! If you want to have another man or two before we're married, you have my permission. It will hurt, but I understand if you want to even the score."

"Permission? I don't need your fucking permission! You think I'm still going to marry you? Hah! I'm going to have EVERY man I desire. It's over Jerry. And this is what I think of you, of us," she said, sliding off her engagement ring and walking into the bathroom.

"That ring cost me two-thousand dollars, I'm still paying for it!" he panicked jumping off of the bed and running into the bathroom just as she dropped it into the toilet.

She flushed it down before he could stop her. Looking him in the *eyes, she said: "Go to hell. I never want to see you again. Get out of my way!"*

He backed away and let her leave. Shame and grief washed over him and he wanted to die on the spot. Then, a wave of nausea attacked him and he vomited into the commode. On the way to her vehicle, she made use of her telekinetic talent and broke all of his car windows and flattened his tires, knowing she could get away with it. Later that evening she stuffed her wedding dress into her fireplace and watched it burn.

She saw him one more time after that fateful day. He came to her house three weeks later and knocked on her door. She was surprised to see him and taken aback because he was sporting a black eye, a swollen lip, and a bandaged cut on his forehead.

"I know you never wanted to see me again, but I need to tell you one last time that I'm so sorry for what I did. I lost the most beautiful, wonderful woman in the world because of my stupid actions, and I hope one day you can forgive me. I still love you, Nina. I always will."

She listened to his apology without saying a word and shut the door in his face.

"Penny for your thoughts?" Luke asked and she jumped out of her trance. He saw the irritated look on her face. "What's wrong?"

"Jerry used to live in this same building, two floors below," she sighed, looking toward the mountains again. "He gave me a key and access card to his apartment too."

Taking her cold hand in his, he said, "Look at me, sweetheart." She turned to face him, and he said, "I'm not Jerry. For the record, I want you to know that I've never had sex with more than one woman at a time. I've been to bachelor parties and seen the exact same thing. I know of two grooms who declined that type of offer because they loved and respected their women too much to stray. And, they are still happily married. When the day comes, and I ask you to be my bride, I will wholeheartedly refuse a bachelor party. I've been a bachelor for a *long* time and since I've fallen in love with you that is the only thing I want to celebrate."

When the day comes? Oh my God! She melted into his arms, her head resting on his chest, "That's music to my ears."

"There's something else I need to tell you," he said. "I feel it's time to come clean."

"Oh. What is it?"

"Shortly after you told me about Jerry's betrayal, I stalked him for a few days and once I got him alone, I roughed him up. I wanted him to know that I didn't like how he hurt you. If he was having second thoughts he should have discussed it with you. I know I scared him, he thought I was going to kill him. I'm not sorry, and I hope that doesn't change things between us," he said, exhaling and feeling anxious.

Joy bubbled up inside of her and she said, "It doesn't change a thing, but it does make me care for you even more. Thank you." She was thrilled that he thought so much of her.

He was relieved that she wasn't angry with him. "You can bring your stuff over here," he said hugging her tight. "Bring anything you want, I'll even let you read my email and text messages. I will be completely transparent."

I think I just fell in love with you. "You don't have to do that. I want to trust you. I'm really looking forward to seeing you more often," she said.

"Me too," he replied, inhaling the fresh scent of her hair.

They left the apartment and drove two miles down the road to Pine Forest Plaza. Walking past the storefronts, they saw one for rent.

"This one looks good. I'll call in the morning and see how much they want for it. This is a great location. There's a big grocery store, several restaurants, a pet store, a beauty shop, and best of all, lots of parking," Luke said.

"I like it too. Will you give me private lessons?" she asked.

"Definitely," he said, clutching her hand. "You've made me a happy man. I'll be forty in April and haven't had a real home since I lived with my parents. There was never any reason to accumulate stuff because I was always on a mission or traveling somewhere. Its past time for me to settle down and every time I came to see you, I felt like I was home. All I need is a comfortable dwelling, three meals a day, and most importantly you, naked, next to me in our bed each night," he said, pulling her close in a bear hug and lifting her off the sidewalk.

Like Nina, Luke preferred simple things and even though he was wealthy, he lived in a modest, sparsely furnished apartment.

"That's a coincidence. My sister turns forty in April too. You don't think you'll get bored living such a quiet life here?" she asked.

"Never," he replied, kissing her and setting her back down on the sidewalk. "Let's get something to eat, I'm starved," he said and they walked into a Chinese restaurant for dinner.

"Woman, you're going to be the death of me," Luke commented, rolling off her as they both struggled to catch their breath.

"I sure hope not," she replied.

"I can't think of a better way to go," he said, and kissed her soundly. "Promise me you'll find out who's after your magic rock tonight."

"I'll slip out and report what I find in the morning," she agreed, yawning.

"Do you ever get too tired to astral?" he asked.

"No. I can go exploring while my body gets a good night's sleep," she said.

"Well, have a safe trip," he said and kissed her again.

"I'll see you in the morning."

She waited until he drifted off to sleep and slipped out of her body.

She didn't want to relive that terrible day; however, she had to find out who was after her precious rock ...

She walks into the sunroom and stands in the corner. Swiping her hand through the air as if she was looking at pictures on a cell phone, she watches the scene unfold and objects start flying.

CRASH!! WHOOP, WHOOP, WHOOP! The sound of windows breaking, the front door bursting open, and the house alarm going off jolted Nina from her altered state when three armed thugs dressed in black stormed into her house; their faces hidden by ski masks. She hears them coming toward the sunroom, is terrified, and objects start flying. A glass vase filled with flowers smashes against the wall next to one of the goons catching him off guard; a piece of broken glass piercing his arm. A wicker chair flies across the room and smacks another thug hard in the face, knocking him off balance. Pictures fall to the floor, and a sharp knife lying on the table flies through the air stabbing the third one in the stomach. He falls to the floor, blood pouring from his wound. She runs out the back door screaming as two thugs follow her. One of them shoots her in the calf, and she falls to the ground.

They grab her by the arms and drag her back to the house.

"What do you want from me?" she asks struggling to break free and crying from the burning pain in her leg.

"Where's your safe?"

"I don't have a safe!"

"Tell me, or I'll blow your pretty head off," the injured thug threat-ened. Before she could answer, they heard sirens closing in.

"We gotta go, man. Shoot the bitch!"

"If I do that, we'll never find it. We didn't go to all this trouble for nothing! We'll be back."

The injured man hits her on the head with his gun, knocking her unconscious and leaves her lying on the floor. They jump in a black van and speed off, leaving a dead man behind.

Nina replays the scene three more times where the injured thug speaks. She listens to his voice but can't place it. "Something about him is familiar. I know him, but I don't know who he is." She feels frustrated and the sound of Luke's snoring in her ear pulls her back into her body ...

He wasn't snoring obnoxiously, just enough to break her concentration. He was lying flat on his back, with one arm wrapped around her. Even though he was sleeping, his hold on her was strong.

She nudged him awake. "You're snoring. Turn over."

He awoke and said, "I'm sorry love." He turned to sleep on his side and she spooned behind him. His hands latched onto hers and they both fell asleep. She wasn't interested in going back to the astral. It was much nicer just holding him.

"What would you like to do today?" he asked, pouring a cup of coffee for her and preparing to cook breakfast. Even though he was ecstatic that she wanted to explore a relationship with him, he wasn't looking forward to spending nights alone in his new apartment. He wanted her next to him every night, but knew he would have to be patient and take it one day at a time.

"I need to go to the feed store," she replied, smiling at him as he set her coffee down in front of her. "Thank you for fixing breakfast. It's not every morning that a hunky, shirtless man wearing only his boxer shorts prepares breakfast for me."

"I'll have to remedy that situation. And, you're welcome," he replied, walking back to the stove to cook a four-cheese and mushroom omelet. She didn't eat meat except for seafood; she loved animals too much to eat them. Admiring his sexy backside, well-developed legs, and wide muscular shoulders, she thought he was physically perfect and seemed taller than six feet. It wasn't just his handsome face and body she adored. She could talk to him about anything; he made her laugh, and they shared a warm, emotional connection. She sipped her coffee thinking that she would probably give in before his six-month lease was up, and let him live with her. She was falling fast against her better judgment. Jerry had never cooked her breakfast, and she rarely invited a lover to her home; wanting to maintain privacy without the danger of them stalking her. Luke had always been the exception to her rules.

Placing their omelets on plates and turning around to carry them to the table, his heart filled with joy when he saw the look of un-abashed adoration on her face … *I think she's falling for me.* "Breakfast is served, my love," he said when she smiled at him.

"It's so nice that you cooked breakfast for me. You're going to spoil me rotten," she stated.

"You've caught on to my plan," he replied winking … *I'd pull the stars down from the sky for you.*

After breakfast, he called to inquire about the storefront for his new studio and scheduled a meeting with the property manager for late in the afternoon. It had been vacant for ten months and he could tell that they were ready to rent it. He was positive he could negotiate a good price.

"Shouldn't you call Bryce before committing to anything?" she asked.

"I know he'll be on board with it. I own twenty-five percent of the company. But you're right. I'll call him now. I want to know how Amber's doing too," he replied, dialing Bryce's number.

"Hey bro," Bryce greeted him.

"Hey. How's Amber?" Luke asked.

"Much better. She's almost back to normal and they'll release her tomorrow. We're going to enjoy a leisurely road trip back to Virginia," he replied. "Are you with Nina?"

"How'd you know?" Luke asked beaming from ear to ear.

"Just a hunch. How's it going with her?"

"Wonderful, and that's what I called to tell you. I'm moving to Charlottesville. I've rented an apartment eight miles from Nina. It was the closest one I could find, and I want to open a martial arts studio here," Luke replied.

"What about your day job?" Bryce asked.

"I quit three weeks ago," he replied.

"And you're just now telling me? That's excellent news!" Bryce exclaimed. "It's about time you settled down. I think it's great, and let me know how much money you need once you find a studio."

"I think I've found one, two miles from my new apartment. I'm meeting with the property manager this afternoon."

"*Unbelievable* ...You don't waste any time!" Bryce laughed. "I'm really happy about this. You know I've wanted to branch out for several years now."

"I'll build our empire down here," Luke replied.

"I'm counting on it. I can't wait to tell Amber the good news," he stated.

"I'll let you go and thanks for the green light," Luke said. "Tell Amber I'm thinking about her."

"I will. Talk to you later," Bryce said ending the call.

Luke looked at Nina. "It's a go."

"Excellent!" she exclaimed.

He helped her feed her animals and then they got into his truck and drove to the Savage Farm and Feed store which was twelve miles from her house. There were two rural, privately owned farm stores within a twenty-five-mile radius and Savage's was the closest. Pulling into the gravel parking lot, Luke recognized a vehicle.

"That's Noah's truck, the black one parked over there," Luke said, pointing to a Ford F250 with a license plate that read GUNS4U. "How's that for coincidence? My stars are aligning perfectly, thanks to you," he said, squeezing her hand.

"Glad I could help," she quipped. "Who's Noah?"

"Don't you remember me mentioning an old friend named Noah Colton?" he asked.

"I remember you saying you had a friend who lived in the area, but I don't recall his name," she replied.

"That's Noah. We talk about once a month. I'd like for you to meet him," he said. "I want to ask him if he'd consider being a martial arts instructor at my new studio."

"Sure. Let's go," she replied.

Noah lived thirty minutes from Nina, in the woods down a dirt and gravel road and up a hill. His home was a two-story log cabin with a wraparound front porch overlooking the mountains. A former Navy SEAL who served with Luke in their younger days, he had been honorably discharged after a head injury left him in a coma for two years. He possessed a strong fighting spirit, and when he emerged from his unconsciousness, the doctors couldn't find anything physically or mentally wrong with him. Outwardly he seemed normal and well-adjusted, and with physical therapy regained his former strength. What no one knew was that his head injury left him with the rare ability to assist lost souls in finding their way to the light. During his nightly astral travels he guided them home. It wasn't difficult because they came to him with no prompting. Even though he was a deeply spiritual man with many secrets, he understood the importance of self-defense and taught firearms safety for a living. He kept up his martial arts training as well.

Luke parked his truck and they walked into the store. Noah was chatting with a store clerk, and turned his head to see who had entered.

"Luke! Hey buddy, what brings you here?" he exclaimed giving Luke a bear hug much to his chagrin. Noah looked at Nina and said, "I do this to embarrass him."

She laughed as he released Luke and said, "I like you already."

Luke shook his head and snickered, "Nice to see you too, Colton."

Noah was ruggedly attractive, standing six feet four inches with shoulder-length blond hair pulled back in a ponytail, light blue eyes, and a muscular body. His skin was perpetually tanned due to spending extended hours outside. A long scar ran down the side of his face and over onto his cheek, marring an otherwise nice-looking face. His wife had died four years earlier after a twelve-year, childless and troubled marriage, and he recently indicated an interest in dating again.

"Who's the lovely lady?" Noah asked grinning at Nina with a sliver of hope that she was unattached.

Luke put his arm around her and replied, "This beautiful lady is Nina Perotti, and she's taken."

Noah laughed and joked, "That's too bad. She could do so much better than you!"

"I have to agree with you old friend," Luke said. "I'm a very lucky man."

"When's the wedding?" Noah asked, teasing him again.

"Whenever the lady wishes," Luke said in a serious tone which didn't go unnoticed by Nina.

"He's renting an apartment at Pine Ridge, and we're going to see how things go," she explained with a racing heart, excited at the possibility of marrying the man of her dreams.

"I'm just joking," Noah said, winking at them.

"I'm glad we ran into you because I'm opening a martial arts studio here, and I need good instructors. Would you consider joining my team?"

"Absolutely. When and where?" he asked.

"There's a vacant storefront at the shopping center down the road from Pine Ridge and I'm meeting with the property manager this afternoon. I'm hoping to sign the lease today. It will be at least two or three months before it officially opens," Luke replied.

"I'm in," Noah stated. "Why don't you two come out to visit?"

"We'd love too," Nina said.

"That sounds great," Luke agreed. "I'll give you a call soon and we'll set a date."

Noah abruptly looked at his watch, "Speaking of dates, I'd better get going. I'm meeting a blind date for lunch. I hope she doesn't stand me up."

"You're a brave man. Who set you up?" Luke asked.

"One of my buddies at the shooting range," he replied.

"Do you know what she looks like?" Luke asked.

"No. It's more fun that way," Noah said. "I know that her name is Roberta and she has short, blond hair."

"You always did have a sense of adventure," Luke remarked.

"It was nice meeting you," Nina said.

"My pleasure, Nina. If he treats you bad, give me a call and I'll straighten him out," Noah teased slapping Luke on the back.

"Have fun!" Luke said as Noah put on his sunglasses and walked out the door, turning and giving them a final wave. Nina smiled, thinking he looked like an intimidating badass you wouldn't want to meet in a dark alley. Although she had a feeling that he was a sweet and laid back guy. She hoped his blind date wouldn't go well. She wanted to introduce him to her sister.

"We should go and get the feed now," Nina said.

"I'll grab a cart," he replied.

They loaded up the cart with enough feed to last three months and rolled it out to his truck. They didn't look up to see Elliott's Jeep entering the parking lot. He was surprised to see them and instantly jealous. He wasn't in the mood to talk to either of them, but there was no way to avoid it.

He parked the Jeep and walked in their direction. "Hello. Funny meeting you two here," he said, trying to be pleasant.

"Elliott! Good to see you," Nina said cheerfully, as Luke tried not to scowl, nodding his head in greeting. "What brings you here?"

"Getting food for Morgan," he replied. Morgan was his horse and at this point in time, his closest friend. "What about you?"

"The same," she replied, feeling a weird vibe coming from him. Something about his demeanor unsettled her.

Luke was arranging the large feed bags in the back of his truck while Nina and Elliott exchanged pleasantries.

"I hear you're moving down here soon. Welcome to the neighborhood," Elliott said to Luke.

"Thanks. I'm looking forward to it," he replied with a half-smile.

"Well, I'll see you later. Have a nice day," Elliott said and walked on into the store.

"You too," Nina replied.

Luke secured the tailgate and they stepped into his truck. "You don't like him, do you?" she asked with an amused expression.

"No, I don't. But he's your friend and as long as he doesn't try anything with you, I'm okay with it," he replied, knowing they would have trouble with him before long.

"I'm sure he won't. Now that he knows about us, he'll probably make himself scarce," she commented.

I can only hope … He thought as they pulled onto the road and he reached over to hold her hand.

Inside the store, Elliott was seething with jealousy. He walked the aisles several times trying to concentrate on what he planned to buy. He remembered Nina said that Luke would be going back to Vienna to get his stuff in about two days. Elliott decided that he would conveniently stop by to see her and bring her the items she left at his house; after calling first to make sure she was alone. This way he could spend time with her and try to change her mind about Luke.

The installers arrived with her new security doors and windows bright and early the following day. Normally, it would have taken several weeks to get the ones she wanted. Fortunately, she knew the owner of the Specialty Door and Window Company, and he had the ones she wanted in stock. She purchased three entry and bullet resistant doors, one for the front entry, one for the kitchen, and one for the sunroom because it opened onto the back patio. She hoped these doors would deter highly skilled attackers using heavy-duty tools such as crowbars, sledgehammers, axes, wedges, saws, steelcutters, and power drills. She replaced all of the windows in her house with security windows providing a similar level of protection. She and Luke watched the installers replace each door and window. It was almost dinnertime when the installation was completed.

"I think that was an excellent decision," Luke said, taking her into his arms.

"Yeah, a very expensive one," she sighed. "After the security system is installed tomorrow, I'll feel even more peace of mind."

"Me too. Then I'll move down here. Since Bryce is out of town, Noah said he would come along and help me move."

"My big, strong, man of muscle can't lift heavy furniture all by himself?" she teased.

"I could, but since he offered I don't mind the help," he replied.

"I'm glad his blind date didn't work out. I want to introduce him to Madison," she said.

He laughed, replying, "Would she move here if they hit it off?"

"Yes. I know she would."

"You could introduce her to Elliott too," he suggested.

She smiled knowing Luke was jealous, "That's a good idea. I'll ask her to visit soon and we'll have a dinner party and introduce her to both of them."

Speaking of dinner, are you getting hungry?" he asked.

"Yes. What would you like to eat?"

"A vegetarian pizza," he replied.

"We could order one half vegetarian and the other with pepperoni and sausage," she said.

"Sounds perfect, like us," he said, kissing her.

The security system technicians arrived at 8:30 the next morning and finished installing her new system five hours later. "I'm all set now," she remarked.

He kissed her and replied, "We better go and pick up the moving truck. Noah's meeting me at the apartment in an hour."

She drove him to pick up the U-Haul and he felt sad leaving her. He would miss her warm body next to him tonight. "Be good while I'm away," he said, walking her back to her SUV.

"You won't be gone very long," she replied.

"I know, but it will seem like an eternity," he sighed.

"Kiss me goodbye," she said, wrapping her arms around his neck.

He kissed her for a good, long while and then gazed into her eyes. "I love you. Be careful until I get back."

"I will. I'll come over and help you set-up your apartment," she replied as he opened the door for her.

"I'm looking forward to that. I'll see you soon, sweetheart," he said, leaning down to kiss her once more.

"Have a safe trip to Vienna," she replied and he closed the door. She waved and he watched her drive away.

He met up with Noah at Pine Ridge and they had a great time driving to Vienna and reminiscing about the past.

She had the rest of the day to herself, and decided to stop by Elliott's house and pick up the belongings she had left there. It wasn't much, just some clothes and personal items, because she thought she would be staying with him until she got her house secured. She never dreamed that Luke would want an exclusive relationship and tell her that he loved her. She smiled driving down the highway thinking about all the fun times ahead and how magical it felt when he said, "I love you."

She pulled into Elliott's driveway and he walked out to greet her. "Hey girl, it's good to see you again!"

"You too. What have you been up to?" she asked, happy to see him.

"Not much. Did you get your house all fixed up?"

"Yes, and it looks so nice. You'd never know that the doors and windows are bullet and break-in resistant."

I have to find another way to get that rock ... "Come on inside and visit for a while," he said.

They walked into his house with the split foyer and up the stairs, settling into comfy chairs in the living room. "So, how's it going with Luke?" he asked.

"So far so good," she replied.

"Don't you think it's happening too fast?"

"No. It's a surprise, but we've known each other a long time. I want to see where it goes. He is uprooting his life and moving down here to be with me. That says a lot."

"You must really care for him. I wish it were me. I have feelings for you too, Nina," he stated in a solemn tone.

She began feeling uncomfortable and was getting those strange vibes from him that she felt earlier at the feed store.

"I'm flattered that you do, but my heart is with Luke," she replied.

"There's nothing I can do to change your mind?"

"No."

"Not even if he breaks your heart?"

"If he breaks my heart, I'm through with men. I'll go back to my old ways, permanently."

"I wouldn't mind being included in your old ways," he stated with a disarming, leering look, undressing her with his eyes.

The thought of having sex with him was suddenly appalling, even though she had fantasized about him from time to time. She had never felt uneasy around him until this moment. These new feelings were alarming and she wanted to go home.

"No more friends with benefits, *ever*," she clarified.

"We don't have to be friends," he remarked jokingly, scratching his upper arm where the glass had cut him when he had attempted to rob her. He kept it bandaged and wore loose fitting shirts to conceal it. An image of one of the masked thugs being stabbed in the arm from flying glass flashed through her mind, but she dismissed it because she wanted to leave.

"What are your plans for tonight? Would you like to have dinner together?" he asked.

"Thank you, but no. I've got some leftovers I need to eat, and then I'm going to relax by the fire and read a book."

"Then go get your things and be on your way!" he demanded in a huff.

"I will," she replied, rising from the chair, disturbed by his sudden change of attitude. He watched her walk down the hallway, scowling and annoyed that she had spurned him.

Entering the room she had stayed in a few nights ago, a heavy, ominous feeling settled in her stomach, and she struggled to keep from vomiting. Something bad was going to happen, and her hands were shaking as she threw her things into the suitcase. She couldn't wait to get out of his house. She saw the beginnings of a vision and blocked it immediately with a psychic shield ... *GO AWAY! I DON'T WANT TO KNOW RIGHT NOW!*

With a wave of her hand, her shield went up and the vision ceased. She took a few deep breaths, picked up her suitcase, and walked back to the living room.

Elliott noticed the change in her demeanor when she returned. "Are you okay? You look pale," he asked rather curtly.

"My stomach feels queasy. I might be coming down with something. I better get going, I don't want to spread my germs and make you sick," she replied.

"Okay. I'll walk you out," he said as she made her way down the stairs.

She couldn't help noticing the sixteen-inch sword with the unique scrollwork on the blade and the red stone hilt displayed prominently on the wall next to the front door ... *I never noticed that before, it looks ancient* ... she paused to take a closer look ... *He must have just put it up* ... She felt an irresistible desire to touch it. Reaching up, she slid her finger along the flat part of the blade, and the image of a woman with long curly black hair, bright blue eyes, and full lips entered her mind. Despite her loveliness, she appeared furious, and ready to lash out at someone. Feeling the woman's rage, she snatched her finger away from the sword. She was used to this type of reaction when she touched an old item. Sometimes the feelings were pleasant, and other times they weren't. She found most items carried impressions from their respective histories.

"I don't mind if you touch it," he said, observing how she recoiled from it.

"I was afraid of cutting my finger," she replied with her back turned, and continued out the door.

He walked the short distance to her vehicle and said, "I'm sorry for being terse with you. I really like you, Nina. I wish I was in Luke's place. But, I understand how you feel about him, and I want to be your friend and someone you can count on. I'm here if you need me."

Feeling a small measure of relief, she looked into his eyes, faked a smile, and replied, "Thanks, Elliott. I hope you enjoy your evening." She got into her SUV, slammed the door, and drove off without waving goodbye. Dejected, he turned and skulked back into his house.

Driving home, she felt the vision returning, and pulled off onto the side of the road until it passed ... *I hate visions. I only see them when something bad is going to happen that will upset my life. Get on with it!* Her body started trembling ...

> *Troubling images flashed before her. She saw Luke being led to a guillotine, and a second before the blade sliced off his head, the vision changed and he was chained naked, face first to a stone wall, being whipped. Her last image was of him lying dead on the ground in a pool of blood ...*

When the vision cleared, she was left in a cold sweat with a pounding heart. The last time she had a vision was two months before she discovered Jerry cheated on her. The visions weren't always clear, although once the event came to pass she would reflect on the premonition and be amazed at the accuracy. She didn't want to believe that she wouldn't marry Jerry, yet the vision of burning her wedding dress and slamming the door in his beaten face was on target. If it had shown him in bed with two women, she would have paid more attention.

Thoughts of Luke's death brought tears to her eyes and a sick feeling in her stomach. She was sobbing before she knew it ... *I have to tell him, I won't be able to hide it and he'll know something's wrong. Oh, Luke, you have to prevent this from happening. We are so good together, and I feel I can really trust you ...* Struggling to regain control of her emotions, she closed her eyes and took several deep breaths, forcing herself to think rationally ... *Who would have a guillotine? Someone out to get him for something he did in his past? The only thing I can do is tell him and listen to what he says. I better get going ...* Wiping away the last of her tears, she merged onto the road and headed home.

Arriving at her house, she was too worried to eat, and decided to try and relax in front of the fire instead. After it was sufficiently stoked, she sank into the chaise lounge and poured a glass of wine. She picked up a medieval romance novel she had been reading, hoping it would take her mind off the vision and transport her to another world. The novel, warm fire, and two glasses of wine made her drowsy, and she fell into a deep sleep. She spent the rest of the night on the lounger, exhausted from worry and the events of the past several days. She missed seeing the text message from Luke telling her goodnight and that he loved her.

Luke was watching TV in his bedroom and listening to Noah snoring in the guest room. He kept checking his phone every ten minutes to see if she would respond to his text. He was disappointed that she didn't reply, and scolded himself for acting like a lovesick teenager. He laid his phone on the nightstand, put in his earplugs, turned off the TV and tried to get some sleep. Tomorrow was going to be a busy day.

Luke and Noah had the U-Haul loaded in three hours. "You weren't kidding when you said you didn't have a lot of stuff," Noah remarked.

"I never felt the need to accumulate things, especially since I was rarely home to enjoy them. I spent my downtime with friends and family whenever I could and used the apartment as a place to sleep, eat, and work out," he replied.

"Does Nina have a lot of stuff?" Noah asked.

"Not an overabundance, but certainly more than I do. Her house feels like a warm and loving home. It's decorated just right."

"Are you planning to marry her?"

"Yes. I'd marry her tomorrow if I could, but she would never go for that. You know I have to prove myself before she'll let me move in," Luke replied.

"She's smart for doing that. From everything you've told me, and meeting her at the feed store, I'd say you've found a wonderful woman to settle down with," Noah stated. "Marriage is work, though — you have to constantly nurture the relationship and not take each other for granted. I tried to do that with Sally, but she was a crazy mess, and I was too blind to see it. I can't believe I took her back twice after she cheated on me and made excuses for her behavior. In spite of all that, I'd like to get married again. I think the right woman is out there, I just haven't met her yet."

"You were too good for Sally. I'm an excellent judge of character, and you married her before I had a chance to meet her and give my seal of disapproval," Luke said.

"Yeah, I won't do that again. The next time I fall madly in love with the wrong woman, I'll let you meet her first," Noah replied laughing.

"It's a deal," Luke answered. "By the way, Nina wants to introduce you to her sister, Madison."

"Is she pretty?"

"From the pictures I've seen, she is. I'm going to meet her family over Thanksgiving and I'll let you know. Nina's adopted, so Madison isn't her biological sister. She looks like your type though, tall with long hair."

"Adoption is good. I'd love to have kids one day, either adopted or my own flesh and blood, it doesn't matter. And I don't have a type. Tall, medium, or petite, long hair or short, I don't care as long as she has a good heart and is sweet and reasonably attractive."

"I think you'll find the right woman soon, and you'll be a great father too," Luke said laughing as they stepped into the U-Haul.

"I hope so. Let's get you back to Charlottesville so you can woo your sweetheart."

Waking up on her chaise lounge, she heard Rogue crowing. She was surprised that she'd spent the night there. Luke would be heading back today, and she expected to hear from him sometime this afternoon. She picked up her phone before getting off the lounger, and smiled when she read his text message from last night: "Wish you were here with me tonight. Can't wait to see you tomorrow. I love you and sweet dreams."

I love you too, Luke. But I'm not ready to tell you yet ... Although she felt he was the one and this time it would be different, a part of her was still afraid that he would break her heart. *Better to make him wonder a little longer and continue falling in love with me.* Thoughts of her chilling visions from yesterday came back to haunt her, casting a shadow on her newfound happiness. She decided to stop dwelling on it and get on with the day she had planned: early morning yoga, breakfast, tending her animals, and cleaning her house. She would be too busy to think of unhappy things, and would talk to Luke about it tonight.

Luke called her at 3:30. "Hey beautiful. I'm here. What are you doing?"

The sound of his voice lifted her spirits and she replied, "You have excellent timing. I just finished cleaning the house."

"Good. Now you can come over to my place and help me move in. You don't have to do any lifting, Noah and I can handle that. I just want to see your lovely face."

Her heart felt light and she answered, "I'll be there soon."

"I can't wait to see you, sweetheart. Drive safe."

"I will."

"Why didn't you ask her what she was doing last night, and if she got your text?" Noah asked with a big grin.

"Because I don't want to sound like a possessive jerk," he replied. "I'll find another way to bring up that topic."

Anticipating that Luke would want her to stay the night, she gathered up some personal items and a change of clothes. Seeing as he had moved down here solely for her, she felt comfortable assuming such but would wait until he asked her to stay.

When she arrived at the apartment complex, Noah and Luke

were securing a sizeable table to a rolling dolly with bungee cords. She parked a few spaces away from the U-Haul and walked over to greet them. Luke paused, watching her walk toward him, and feeling giddy, while Noah stood by, amused at the change in his friend.

Holding out his arms, he greeted her with a tight bear hug. "How's my lady?"

"Doing just fine," she replied, as he gently released his hold to look at her. Although she was smiling sweetly at him, he could tell that something was bothering her. He read it in her eyes, a look of worry *... I hope she isn't having second thoughts.* He decided to tease her to see if that was on her mind.

"I hope you haven't changed your mind about us," he teased and kissed her cheek. "But, if you have, I can turn around and go back."

"Heavens no!" she exclaimed, swatting him playfully. "I'm not letting you go that easily."

"Just checking," he replied, feeling reassured. He would find out what was bothering her later tonight.

It took them a little over three hours to get Luke moved in. The guys moved the heavy furniture and Nina carried smaller boxes, groceries, and set up his kitchen and dresser drawers. He invited Noah to join them for dinner, and called Antonio's Italian Eatery for delivery.

After Noah left, Luke pulled Nina into his arms and kissed her like there was no tomorrow. Their passion was overwhelming, and he picked her up and carried her into his bedroom where they made love for the next two hours.

Holding her close after the loving, she was unusually quiet and the mood felt heavy. "What's wrong honey?" he asked, running his fingers through her hair.

"I had a vision of something bad," she replied, loosening their embrace to face him.

"Was I in it?"

"Yes."

"Well, if you saw me with another woman, then your vision is dead wrong," he stated.

"That's not it. I saw your death," she replied, blinking back tears.

"Oh. So, how am I going to die?" He'd faced death more times than he could count without fear. And yet, a feeling of trepidation formed in his chest.

She explained her devastating vision of his death which led to more questions.

"A guillotine? That seems out of place in this day and time. Do you think it might be something from a past life?" he asked.

"Possibly. The visions aren't always clear," she replied. "Do you have any enemies that might have a guillotine or a dungeon where they could torture someone?"

"Probably, but I don't know which ones," he sighed, kissing her. "We can't dwell on this. I'm not a psychic, but I know that the more you worry about something the more you run the risk of attracting it. Maybe your vision is just a warning. I'm always aware of my surroundings, and I've decided I'm not going to die anytime soon. I have too much to live for, meaning *you*. Please tell me if you see anything else. In the meantime, I want to enjoy you all night long. You turn me on like no one ever has, and I'm crazy in love with you. For me, there's no turning back."

She responded by kissing him and pressing her hips against his growing excitement, igniting more fevered lovemaking until they succumbed to exhaustion and fell asleep.

There was no rooster to wake them, and they slept until 7 a.m., which they considered late. She awoke first, remembering their incredible night of passion, and realizing that she never got her personal items out of her vehicle last night. Not wanting to disturb him, she slowly slipped out of his arms and started getting dressed. She put one leg into her jeans when he opened his eyes and asked, "Leaving so soon?"

She smiled replying, "No. I was just getting dressed enough to go out to my car and get my stuff."

He sat up and said, "You don't need to. I bought some things for you to keep here."

Her eyebrows shot up in surprise and she replied, "Really? No man has ever done that for me. Thank you." She was tickled by his thoughtfulness.

"Well, I'm not just any guy," he declared, getting out of bed. Putting on his robe and walking into the closet, he took a flannel shirt off its hanger and gave it to her. "Wear this until we take a shower. I don't want you to be cold, and you'll look unbelievably sexy in my shirt."

She hugged him. "I need to put on my socks. My feet are freezing."

He squeezed her. "I took care of that, too."

She put on his flannel shirt and it felt like a warm caress against her cold body. It was much too large for her and hung down to her knees. She rolled up the sleeves which extended a few inches past her hands.

"Yep, you look hot," he remarked, reaching for a box on a high shelf. "I hope you like these."

She opened the box and her face lit up. Luke had bought her a pair of pink bootie slippers in a suede-like material. The inside was lined with lamb's wool. "They're wonderful!" she exclaimed throwing her arms around him. "Thank you."

"Put them on before you touch me with your icy feet," he joked. "I know pink is your favorite color."

"Yes." She was smiling as she slipped into them. "They feel like heaven. Thank you so much. When did you have time to shop for these?"

"I needed new slippers. The ones I had look like someone's dog munched on them. We stopped by a mall on the way here, and I bought a new pair for myself. Noah saw these pink ones and brought them to me saying he'd found me the perfect pair of slippers. I thought they would be perfect for you and so I bought them," he explained.

"Let me fix you breakfast," she offered, wanting to do something for him in return.

"It's a deal. I'm famished," he said, reaching for a large bag which was on a lower shelf. "I hope I got the right things. Check and see."

He handed her the bag, and when she looked inside she saw a pink toothbrush, toothpaste, mint-flavored dental floss, bottles of her favorite shampoo and conditioner, her preferred deodorant, a bottle of rosewater spray that she liked to use on her face after showering, and a bar of luxury soap. He even included a can of hairspray. She liked using it to keep her bangs in place. In that moment, her lingering worries about their budding relationship vanished. Luke was a man who paid attention to the things she liked, the little things that showed how much he cared. She had never told him her shoe size, so she figured he must have picked up a pair of her shoes to find out. She was so touched by his thoughtfulness that the words rolled off her tongue before she had time to think: "I love you." She gasped, putting her hand over her mouth and looking at him with wide eyes.

Joy overwhelmed him and he took her in his arms and said, "I must have bought the right things. You know I love you too." He was surprised and elated to hear those words from her this soon. It was more than he had hoped for, and he thought the way she announced it was cute and endearing. They held each other for a few moments until his stomach growled and then they burst out laughing.

"Still think I'm sexy?" he asked.

"You are the sexiest man alive, and I need to fix you breakfast now. What would you like?"

"Pancakes. I haven't had pancakes in ages. I bought a multigrain mix that I think you'll like," he said. "And strawberries too. I know they're your favorite fruit."

"Another sweet thing you remembered! I put them in the refrigerator yesterday. I love pancakes so this will be a treat for both of us."

"I want to help. What would you like for me to do?" he asked as they walked into the kitchen.

"You can start the coffee and I'll make the pancakes," she replied, smiling and kissing him.

"If you keep doing that we'll end up back in bed for the rest of the day," he remarked.

They went about preparing breakfast, engaging in casual chit-chat about ordinary things. He thought this would be a good time to ask her what she did yesterday after he left.

"So, how much fun did you have while I was gone?" he jested.

"Absolutely none," she sighed, her tone of voice sounding distressed. "I stopped by Elliott's house to pick up my things, the same things sitting outside in my car at the moment."

He felt a sharp stab of jealousy which he deftly concealed and asked, "Did something happen?"

"Yes. He indicated his interest in me and leered at me like I was a juicy steak. I told him that you had my heart and he still tried to come on to me. He seemed like a different person and all I wanted to do was leave. He wanted me to stay for dinner, and when I declined his offer he told me to get my things and leave. He sounded angry. I walked down the hall to get my stuff and my body started shaking and the vision started. I pushed it aside, got my things and left. He walked me out to my car and apologized for being terse to me. He said he still wanted to be my friend, but I don't want any more to do with him. He gives me the creeps now," she said, shaking her head.

"Did he try to force himself on you?" Luke asked with a look that said he wanted to strangle Elliott.

"No. Even if he tried, I can defend myself. It wouldn't be the first time I've kicked a man in the nuts or sent an item sailing across the room to smack him in the head."

He breathed a sigh of relief and was glad that she no longer wanted to remain friends with Elliott. "I know you can take care of yourself, but my protective instincts are heightened around you. I guess I won't beat him up now," he kidded with a wink. "However, if he tries anything again, watch out."

She laughed, hugging him.

"You can't go around beating up every man who takes an interest in me."

"You're right. There are too many," he joked.

"If we had a daughter, the poor girl wouldn't be allowed to date until she's forty!" she stated.

"Forty-five. We've never discussed it, but how do you feel about having children?" he asked releasing her so he could look at her face.

"I like children, and wouldn't mind having one or two. But if it never happens that's okay. It won't be the end of the world for me. What about you?"

"I like kids too. I think it would be fun, and I know we would have beautiful and smart children. However, I agree with you. If it happens for us that would be wonderful, but if not, we have each other and that's enough for me," he said.

"Me too. We'll leave it up to fate," she replied.

Luke and Nina worked out a plan to see each other every day and still have space to do their own thing. They enjoyed each other's company too much to sleep alone at night and decided to continue spending nights and mornings together, and then take care of whatever tasks they needed to accomplish during the day. Luke had much work to do with getting Decker Martial Arts up and running. There was the matter of filing the necessary paperwork and handling other legalities; planning a marketing and hiring campaign; and modifying the storefront. Nina had her animals, some psychic work for the Agency that required intense concentration, and time to play her guitar, read a book, or work out.

Thanksgiving was fast approaching, and Nina's family was excited to meet the man she adored. They were overjoyed that she had found someone worthy of her and hoped he wouldn't turn out to be a disappointment. Her parents had liked Jerry, although there was something about him which irked her mother and he never had her full approval. Nina's appreciation and love for her adopted family ran deep. While loading the washing machine, she reflected back upon her nightmarish childhood before she met them.

Orphaned as a baby, she had grown up in the foster care system being transferred from family to family because she was deemed a problem child no one could handle for more than a year or two. She was shy, introverted, and to an extremely religious foster family, the devil's spawn. She was highly sensitive and her emotions manifested in unusual ways, scaring most people. In times of acute emotional distress, pyrokinesis had often taken over, and she had inadvertently started fires or blew up things. Her abilities had gradually developed over time, becoming stronger as she grew older.

In her early teenage years, she had been placed with a kind family, Gabe and Claire Perotti, whom she had bonded with, and they had adopted her. They both worked at a nearby high school. Gabe was a guidance counselor and Claire taught music. They had one biological daughter, Madison, and they had become best friends, as they were two years apart. Claire had encouraged Nina to explore music, and she learned to play the guitar. Nina was blessed with a beautiful singing voice, and the four of them had spent many evenings singing in the family room while Claire played the piano.

Her adoptive mother practiced white witchcraft, and possessed some psychic ability, as did Madison. She taught her daughters how to use the craft to overcome obstacles and better their lives. Madison was enthralled with and practiced formal witchcraft more than Nina. She loved the ceremonial aspects because the preparation provided her with the focus she needed to obtain her goals. Nina didn't like the fuss and pomp of ceremony and preferred focusing on the desired outcome while raising her energy to get results.

Gabe was supportive and loving, helping Nina come out of her shell and establish goals in life. They were instrumental in helping her learn to control her extraordinary abilities. They remained close, Nina going home every Thanksgiving and Christmas and staying in touch via weekly phone calls. She no longer considered them her adoptive parents – they were her only parents.

She had given Luke a key and alarm code to her house and was pleasantly surprised when she heard him call out, "Honey, I'm home!"

"I'm in the laundry room," she called back, closing the lid on the washer and walking out to see him. He was carrying a bouquet of colorful Gerbera daisies.

"I thought these would like nice on your kitchen table," he said.

"They're so pretty!" she enthused, reaching out to embrace him. He greeted her with a long and sensual kiss.

"Thank you for the flowers. You are a sweetheart. I wasn't expecting you for another two hours," she said.

"I finished my to-do list early. Do you want me to leave and come back?" he asked.

"No, this is a wonderful surprise," she replied kissing him again.

"Am I interrupting anything?"

"Just laundry," she laughed.

"Get me dirty so I'll need washing too," he said with a gleam in his eye.

"My pleasure. Let me put these flowers in a vase and then we will both get dirty," she replied giggling. He followed her into the kitchen and once the flowers were set in a vase, they retreated to the bedroom and became extremely dirty.

Two days later, Luke and Nina used the magic rock to teleport to her parents' home for Thanksgiving. He was awestruck when they appeared in her parents' living room, and he hadn't felt a thing; it was as easy as blinking. Claire, Gabe, and Madison approved of Nina's new love, and could see how much he cherished her.

CHAPTER 2

Storm Clouds Gather

After Thanksgiving, when the holiday season jumped into full swing, it seemed to Elliott that everywhere he went he would run into Luke and Nina. He saw them at the Chinese restaurant near Luke's storefront, the grocery store, the hardware store, the local bar, and the movie theatre. It reminded him of what he couldn't have, Nina and her enchanted rock. He coveted the rock more than her, although he missed her attention and the friendship they once shared. He did his best to avoid seeing them and most of the time they never knew he was around. There were a few times when he was forced to acknowledge them and engage in polite small talk. Luke was congenial and discovered that they were both avid football fans. However, Luke was being friendly for Nina's sake in an attempt to get to know his enemy. Neither man liked the other. Nina was civil, yet distant during these encounters and he knew it was from the night he made his feelings known and she rejected him. He could tell she was uneasy in his presence. What Elliott didn't know was that every time Nina saw him, the image of the frantic black-haired woman entered her mind shouting ... *STAY AWAY FROM HIM!* This prompted her to tell Luke about the ancient sword hanging on Elliott's wall and her impression of the agitated woman. Luke believed this was confirmation that Elliott was up to something. Nina silently thanked the ghostly woman for her warnings and wondered how she was connected to the old sword and where Elliott bought it. She attempted making contact with this woman on the astral plane and was unsuccessful.

The first weekend in December, the rural co-op hosted a Christmas Party at an extravagant farmhouse, where Elliott endured seeing Luke and Nina together again. He almost didn't attend the party and decided to go at the last minute because there were other co-op members he wanted to see. Like before, the three of them were cordial with each other for a short time and then dispersed to chat with others. Nina was a bit friendlier to Elliott even though the ghostly woman screamed at her again. Elliott thought Nina looked beautiful tonight in her fitted black velvet dress which fell slightly above her knees, black stockings and high heels. The dress was low-cut, sleeveless, and she wore a bright red shawl around her shoulders. She was the prettiest woman in the room. He kept a discreet eye on the two of them as they mingled with other guests. The sight of Luke and Nina being joyful with each other, holding hands, gazing into each other's eyes, dancing, and laughing and joking with others was really bothering him tonight. He hated her happy glow and felt it should belong to him. It was obvious to Elliott that their relationship wouldn't be ending any time soon, unless he helped it along. He continued observing them while hatching a new plan to obtain the enchanted rock. First, he would have to get rid of Luke; her guard dog protector who was built like a fortress. He knew the only way he could take him down would be to kill him from a distance. Although Elliott was in good physical shape he couldn't best Luke in a fight.

Luke and Nina left the party before midnight and drove back to her house. "So, did you have a nice time?" she asked.

"Yes. I always have a nice time with you. Doesn't matter where we go or what we do," he replied taking her hand.

"I'm going to put up the Christmas tree tomorrow. Would you like to help?" she asked.

"Of course. That's something couples should do together. I'm glad we're a couple," he said lifting her hand and kissing it while keeping his eyes on the road. "I can't believe I forgot to tell you this, but I got a text from Bryce earlier and he's going to ask Amber to marry him tomorrow."

"That's wonderful! Do you think she'll say yes?"

"I know she will, and she'll want to get married in the spring or summer in grand style with a cast of hundreds," he exaggerated with a laugh.

"I'm already looking forward to their wedding!"

"Speaking of weddings … what kind of wedding do you want one day?" he asked with apprehension, wanting to know but hoping she wouldn't take his question the wrong way and think he was rushing things.

She smiled sensing his anxiety and replied, "I want a small wedding with no more than seventy-five guests, two bridesmaids, and a drop dead gorgeous dress. That probably sounds silly coming from a tomboy farm girl, but I enjoy dressing up now and then, like for the party we just attended."

"As luscious as you look in that dress, I can't wait to take it off of you," he started grinning.

"We still have thirty-five more minutes until we get home. You'll just have to tough it out," she teased.

"Sweet torture, that's what you do to me," he replied.

When they arrived home he wasted no time carrying her into the bedroom and taking off her little black dress. They slipped beneath the sheets for a zesty session which left them too exhausted for a second go round.

"I think you've worn out this old man," he joked, pulling her close to spoon in front of him.

"I'm pretty beat myself," she replied. "I think we should get some sleep."

"Me too. Good night my love," he said wrapping his arms around her.

"Good night, and thank you for going to the party with me."

"My pleasure, sweetheart. Anything for you."

She wasn't planning to venture to the astral tonight, however, her body had other plans and she lifted out with no effort. Since she was up and out, she thought this would be a good time to go looking for the goons who broke into her house ...

Her astral body appears in the sunroom and she relives the frightening experience once again, yet this time she is determined to re-watch certain portions until she identifies the intruders. She replays the masked brute telling her to show him the safe.

"Where's your safe?"

"I don't have a safe!"

"Tell me or I'll blow your pretty head off," the injured thug threatened. Before she could answer, they heard sirens closing in.

"We gotta go, man. Shoot the bitch!"

"If I do that, we'll never find it. We didn't go to all this trouble for nothing! We'll be back."

The injured man hits her on the head with his gun, knocking her unconscious and leaves her lying on the floor. They jump in a black van and speed off, leaving a dead man behind.

She suddenly recalls Elliott scratching his upper arm the last time she was at his house and asks the universe, "Show me what the intruders were doing before they covered their faces."

What she saw next was a shocking revelation. Elliott and two other men were at his house discussing preparations for the robbery.

"Are you guys ready?" Elliott asked. The three of them were dressed in black and hadn't put on their ski masks yet. "Please tell me that van parked outside is untraceable."

"It's stolen and the VIN is scratched off. We can abandon it if something goes wrong. Now, let's get on with it," the heavyset guy who died on her floor said with annoyance.

"I can't wait to see this magic rock," the third thug stated as they walked out of Elliott's house and got into the black van.

She feels a mixture of shock and deep hurt. "I thought he was my friend. He was at my hospital bedside, holding my hand when I came out of the coma, which he caused!"

While she thinks back on the good times she spent with Elliott, scenes appear in front of her like the fun times they had together riding their horses, great conversations, going hiking, rock climbing, and whitewater rafting with mutual friends from the co-op, the way he cared for her and her animals when she was in the hospital ... the hospital that he put her in! She converses with herself, and when she thinks each thought, the answers appear before her.

"How did he find out about the rock? I was cloaked as a Pitbull when I took it ... Oh no, he's an astral traveler too ... That son of a bitch! He looked at my past when I made those stacks of cash! HOLY SHIT!"

Her thoughts place her in Elliott's bedroom and she watches him sleep. "I can see that he's dreaming ...Well, that fucking asshole is going to have an epic nightmare." She jumps into his dream taking the form of a giant wolf.

Elliott turns and runs when he sees the wolf from Hell barreling toward him. He runs until he is out of breath and falls hard to the ground. The wolf tears into his leg and he screams so hard he wakes up covered in sweat and gasping for air. He throws off the covers and sees bite marks and blood oozing down his lower right leg.

"CHRIST!" he swears, as a heavy picture mounted on his bedroom wall crashes to the ground. He gets out of bed and runs toward the bathroom intending to bandage his bleeding leg when the bathroom mirror shatters and shards of glass fall to the floor. While objects in *his bedroom go airborne and crash into the wall, he does a quick job of disinfecting and bandaging his leg. He carefully walks back to his bed trying not to trip over the items on the floor, sobbing and pleading over and over "Nina, I'm so sorry, please forgive me. I promise I'll never bother you again."*

She replies even though he can't hear her, "I could kill you right now and I've half a mind to do it!" Her final flash of anger starts a fire in the corner of his room and he races into the hallway for the fire extinguisher.

"I'm done here," she says, and returns to her body ...

Lying in bed, she thinks of Elliott's betrayal. Luke has turned over and is lying flat on his back, sleeping peacefully. Her mind is racing and she can't fall back asleep. She gets out of bed, puts on her robe and goes into the sunroom. Sitting on the overstuffed, wine-colored sofa, she props her feet up on the matching ottoman and tears start falling. Luke wakes up ten minutes later and sees that she isn't next to him. Getting out of bed, he walks to the kitchen ... *I bet she's in the sunroom* ... he enters and hears her sniffling. He sits down next to her, taking her in his arms.

"What's wrong, love?"

"It was Elliott," she replied. "He broke into my house with his goons."

"I knew that guy was trouble the moment I met him," Luke answered hugging her closer. "What are you going to do?"

"I entered his dreams as a giant wolf and attacked him. When he woke up, he had bite marks and blood running down his leg. I trashed his bedroom, broke a mirror, and started a fire," she replied. "I thought he was a friend. I knew he was hiding something, but I never would have dreamed he was after the rock. I wasn't careful when I first started working with it ... and now it's recorded on the astral for anyone who wishes to investigate. He's an astral traveler too, and knows how to view the past. Even with my abilities, I don't like to pry into the dark areas of others pasts. The ghostly woman was right in warning me. I only wish she had appeared sooner."

"You might want to consider doing background checks on *all* of your friends and acquaintances. You're welcome to investigate me, if you haven't already. There's plenty of questionable things back there, but I want you to know that I've always been honest with you and like I said before, I don't want any secrets between us," he stated letting go to look in her eyes. "When you hurt, I hurt. And, I have no problem ridding the world of scum like him."

She laughed a little and replied, "I don't know where to go from here. We can't go to the police … they might lock me up for being crazy. He knew I was there and kept apologizing and saying he would never bother me again. I wish I could believe it, but I don't."

"Do you want me to take care of him? I can make him disappear."

"Thank you, but no. I don't want to live with that on my conscience. After my first and only assassination all those years ago, I swore never to kill anyone again. Too much emotional aftermath to contend with, even though he was a wicked, despicable man," she said with a tired sigh. "However, I'm older and stronger now, and if Elliott does anything else, I'll reconsider. Do what you want to him and don't tell me," she replied, laying her head on his chest. "That's the only secret you're allowed to keep from me."

He kissed the top of her head and asked, "Do you want to go back to bed?"

"Yeah, a few more hours of sleep will be good."

They got up from the sofa and back into bed. Nestling into each other, the warmth of his body soothed her nerves and lulled her to sleep within a few minutes.

"If I get the chance, I'm going to kill the asshole," he whispered.

Elliott survived the night and extinguished the fire in his bedroom before it did too much damage. He cleaned up the aftermath of hurricane Nina and checked the rest of the house for further damage. He was relieved to find the melee was confined to his bedroom. He was still in a state of shock over Nina's abilities ... *I want to disappear until things calm down, although, there's no hiding from someone who can find you from the astral. I'm not giving up on the rock. I have to catch her unaware and that's okay ... I've got plenty of time.* He kept telling himself that and trying not to worry about her telekinetic and astral talents. He packed his belongings and made arrangements to stay at a hotel forty-five miles down the road. However, he couldn't just up and leave. He had to board his horse, Morgan, a friendly Palomino he was going to miss. He reflected on fun times when he and Nina would ride their horses together. Buttercup and Morgan were great friends ... *Like we once were.* He knew that leaving town wouldn't keep Luke or Nina from finding him. There was truly no place to hide. Still, he wanted to get out of town for a while.

He took Morgan to another friend's ranch for care, making up the lie that he had to leave to take care of some family business due to a recent inheritance.

"I appreciate you looking after Morgan. I don't know how long I'll be gone, but you know how to get in touch with me," Elliott said to Judd Slater, an avid horse lover who would enjoy having Morgan around.

"My pleasure, take as long as you need. I'm surprised that you're not leaving him with Nina," he replied.

"Yeah, things have changed with her. She has a full-time lover now and I don't want to impose on her. He's the possessive type and doesn't like me," Elliott replied rolling his eyes.

"That's unfortunate, but life happens," he said. "Have a safe trip and give me a call when you want to come and get him."

"I will. Thanks again," Elliott said and walked back to his truck.

He didn't mind leaving Morgan with Judd and if something happened to him, he knew Judd would take ownership of Morgan and treat him well. Once he stole the magic rock, he could disappear for good. He knew he had to kill both Luke and Nina to have any lasting peace. He spent a good deal of time contemplating different scenarios on how he could kill Nina and frame Luke for it while holding the sword for inspiration. However, framing Luke for her murder would take more time and energy than he wanted to expend. He scratched that plan and came up with an easier one. Luke would be his first target.

Nina spied on Elliott from the astral every day, knowing he was still plotting to steal the rock. She swore to remain vigilant and ruin his efforts. She took great pleasure in troubling him from time to time by moving objects around, smashing things, and terrorizing his dreams. As Christmas drew closer, she became distracted with the fun of the season and stopped aggravating him. He returned to his house on New Year's Eve.

Luke and Nina spent Christmas with each other's families by using the enchanted rock to teleport back and forth. Luke formally introduced her to Bryce and Amber, his cousin Jenny and her husband Zac and their children. They welcomed her with open arms, happy that Luke had found someone special. Bryce and Amber knew her from the astral realm, and meeting in person was like reuniting with long-lost friends.

When the holiday rush was over they reveled in a quiet New Year's Eve, welcoming the New Year in each other's bodies in front of a roaring fire. After the loving, they remained wrapped around each other and talked about the future. Luke's new studio was scheduled to open the first week in March. He still needed to hire instructors and had a few interviews lined up for the third week in January. He had high expectations for his new instructors and looked forward to testing their abilities. Noah was helping him with this and quickly becoming his right-hand man.

"The holidays were fun, but I'm glad they're over," he said. "I'm looking forward to getting the studio up and running."

"Me too. I think it's exciting," she replied.

"I've got a meeting with someone from the leasing office the day after tomorrow to go over a few more changes I want to make to the space. But for the most part, I'm glad the actual construction to get it where I want it is less than I anticipated," he said.

"Come and kiss me goodbye; I'm off to my meeting," Luke said zipping up his heavy jacket and putting on his knit cap.

"They're calling for snow this afternoon, I want you to start heading home at the first flake," she stated.

"I know how to drive in the snow, better than most. Besides, if I ever got into a bad situation, you would find me and teleport me home," he said. "And the truck too."

"You're right, I would," she replied smiling.

"I should be back around 12:30. Do you want me to bring lunch?"

"Yes, I'd like that."

He pulled her close and kissed her. "I still can't get enough of you."

"I can't get enough of you either."

He kissed her again and said, "I love you, woman. I'll give you a call when I'm on my way home."

"I love you too," she replied. "Drive safe."

"Always," he said with a wink and closed the front door.

She watched him walk to his truck, get in, and drive away ... *I'm a lucky lady.* She had the morning to herself and planned to use the time to write a song which was running through her mind. It was a love song for Luke and she wanted to serenade him on Valentine's Day next month. Picking up her guitar and a pad of paper, she retreated to the sunroom to get started.

The day was exceptionally cold, gray, and quiet, with the smell of impending snowfall. Elliott was wearing a heavy, wool stadium coat with an attached hood. His New Year's resolution was to get rid of Luke as soon as possible. He wasn't able to spy on them like he wanted from the astral because he kept seeing the same old thing. It didn't take him long to conclude that Nina was able to cloak herself and her home with a repetitive mirage. Today was the day he would make his move. He was certain his strategy would be a success. He had thought long and hard on the situation while holding the knife and the mental images which entered his head revealed how it should be done. In addition, he had let his emotions run wild and envisioned Luke suffering great torture at his hands. He anticipated backlash from Nina once she found out what he did, however, he was ready for her and had planned accordingly.

He watched discreetly as Luke and two other men emerged from the storefront. Elliott had his hood up and was standing behind a large pillar listening to their conversation. Luke walked with them to the curb, the men said their goodbyes, shook hands, and Luke strolled back to his studio to lock up. Then he watched Luke walk to the grocery store and followed him. Luke entered the store heading to the floral department and stopping to look at long stemmed roses. A female store clerk walked up to him and said, "I was just getting ready to discount these. For the next two days, you can buy a dozen roses for $9.99."

"That's exactly what I'm going to do," he replied, picking up a bouquet of red roses.

"For a special lady?" she asked.

"Yes, very special, and soon to be my wife," he said.

"Are you going to propose tonight?" she asked.

"No, not tonight, but soon. These are just because," he answered. He loved spoiling Nina by bringing her things whenever he went to the store alone. He would bring back her favorite food items and other things he noticed that she needed, or things he thought she might like. She never failed to thank him with a kiss and a smile.

"What a romantic man you are. I'm sure she will love them. I can ring you up over here," the clerk said cheerfully, leading him to her counter which was separate from the main registers.

Elliott pretended to be interested in some flowers close to the counter and as soon as Luke turned toward the counter and the clerk focused on the transaction to ring up his purchase, he came up from behind and stabbed Luke in the back; he vanished into thin air.

The clerk looked up seconds later and said, "Where did he go?"

"I don't know, but he took the roses with him," Elliott replied, noticing a clean counter and no roses in sight.

The clerk looked around in shock and said, "Damn he's fast! I wish they would put a security camera in this department."

"I knew he was standing there, but I was looking at the carnations and didn't see him leave," he said.

"Are you ready to check out?" she asked.

"Not yet, I'm still looking and trying to pick out something nice for my mother."

"Okay. I'll be over there when you're ready," she said, pointing to a section of potted plants.

Elliott continued feigning interest in flowers and casually strolled out of the store … *It worked!* He wanted to do a happy dance. His number one enemy and obstacle was banished to an alternate dimension from which there was no escape, except for death. *I'll send Nina there too, after I steal the rock.*

Nina was wrapped up in writing her new song when she was suddenly overcome with a feeling of dread. Glancing at the clock, it said 1:30 ... *He should be home by now, or at least have called me.* She called his cell and her heart fell when she heard his voicemail greeting. She didn't leave a message and tried calling him again fifteen minutes later. Closing her eyes she inhaled deep breaths, attempting to calm the rising panic so she could slip to the astral and find him. She slid out a few minutes later and checked his apartment, then she stood in the strip mall parking lot next to his truck. The snow was falling and picking up momentum ... *Something's seriously wrong here.* She checked inside the locked storefront and he wasn't there; it was time to do some investigating ...

"Luke, where are you?" she asked the universe. For the first time in her life white, solid walls appeared around her. Using her energy she dissolved the walls and was left standing and staring into total darkness. "I can't believe this!" She surrounded herself with white light and was back inside the storefront. "What happened to Luke?" she asked, swiping her hand in the air and wound up jolting herself back into her body...

"What's going on?" she moaned. The panic she felt earlier seized her with full force, and she was paralyzed with fear and unable to think for almost thirty minutes. She gradually emerged from her catatonic state and mustered enough energy to retrieve the magic rock from its hiding place. With trembling hands, she opened the wooden box and was shocked to discover that the engagement ring Luke had created with his thoughts was gone.

"Where did he go? Why can't I see what happened to him?" The logical part of her mind took control and she forced the fear and anxiety aside. Afraid she might be losing her abilities, she held the rock in her hand, quieted her mind and thought of Luke. In an instant her astral body was back inside the storefront staring out the window, watching the snowfall and no sign of him. *Please, please, show me where he is!* She begged and nothing happened.

She thought of Bryce and saw him in his office in Old Town Alexandria, sitting at his desk and engaged in a discussion with two of his employees. She felt herself materializing into solid form and was unable to stop. Luckily, his employees were sitting in chairs facing him and didn't see her appear. Thankfully, his office was large. She quickly tiptoed behind a small conference table on the other side of the room and hid, placing the rock inside the pocket of her cardigan.

Bryce saw Nina materialize behind the two people talking to him, and his blue eyes grew wide, and he let out a startled gasp.

"You look like you've just seen a ghost!" Ricky Wong, his assistant director said with a laugh.

"Yeah, boss, what's up?" Melinda Ruiz, his receptionist chimed in.

"I just remembered an important call I need to make. We'll finish this discussion later. I'm onboard with your idea and you have my permission to make it happen," he responded with a calmness he didn't feel and his heart pounding.

Melinda and Ricky left his office and Bryce closed the door. "Okay, it's safe to come out. How in the world did you get here?" he asked.

She stood up and walked over to his desk, seating herself in the chair Ricky vacated and bursting into tears.

"What's wrong?" he asked with concern and surprise.

"Luke's vanished!" she cried.

"Vanished how?"

"He's gone! He went to meet with the construction guys about what needs to be done for the new studio and said he'd be back around

12:30. He was supposed to call me before he headed home and he never showed up. I checked the astral, searching for him and I was blocked by solid walls. I dissolved them and was left with nothing but complete darkness. I surrounded myself with white light and when I moved my hand to view the events leading up to his disappearance, I was shoved back into my body. I know something bad has happened to him and I feel helpless because I can't find out where he is," she lamented. "His truck was still in the parking lot and the storefront was locked up. He's nowhere to be found."

Bryce was silent for a few moments. He was astounded at Nina's sudden appearance and disturbed by what she just told him, his brother was missing. He couldn't imagine going to the astral and being met with solid walls and total darkness, especially with her level of talent. Not every astral traveler could go wherever they wanted without restraint.

He looked her in the eyes and said, "I don't know what to think. It's not like him to be anything other than punctual. If he says he will call, he will. My brother keeps time in his head; he's always been a walking clock. I will check the astral tonight and see if I can find him, and ... *how* did you get here in the flesh? You must tell me the secret of teleportation!"

He looks so much like Luke. They have the same handsomely chiseled face, muscular body, and shaved head. If he was a little bit shorter with dark eyes and tanned skin, I would probably lose it. Standing up and reaching into her pocket, she pulled out the rock, placed it in her palm and said, "This is the secret to teleportation. It does other things too."

"Where did you get it?" he asked wanting to hold the rock but fearing he might end up in a strange place. Luke told him that Nina owned an unusual, highly valuable item which Elliott was after and that he was the one who broke into her house. Bryce never imagined it would be an ordinary looking rock with magical powers. As Nina spoke, he noticed a long, red gash forming around her neck.

"On a mission, several years ago. It wanted to come home with me. I have to be careful with it. If I'm holding it and think of certain people or places for more than a minute or two, I will find myself there. Like what you just witnessed. It can help me do and create amazing things, but it won't lead me to … Luke." She choked on his name and more tears streamed down her cheeks.

Bryce placed a box of tissues in front of her. He was compassionate and wanted to help, "Use the whole box if you need to. Don't hold back. Whatever has happened to him, I'm sure was beyond his control. He would never just up and leave you. He's crazy in love with you. We must keep trying to find him. I know you two have been involved with all manner of top secret and unmentionable things and dealt with God only knows what types of bad guys. Someone is out to get him. Do you think Elliott might have something to do with this?"

She was surprised that Bryce mentioned Elliott. "Like how? I don't think he has any psychic abilities other than being able to astral travel, and physically, Luke could beat the shit out of him in two minutes. I don't see how anyone could blindside Luke. Although, Elliott is after my rock."

"Don't be surprised if there is more to Elliott than you know. If he can get Luke out of the way, there's no telling what he will try to do to you. After the incident with Mike Collins, I don't think we should underestimate *anybody*. When you go back to the astral, see what Elliott was doing today. That might help us find Luke," he replied. "I'll do the same."

"I feel like such an idiot, I should have done that in the first place. I panicked because I had such a bad feeling about Luke and visions of his … death when we first got together," she moaned, shaking her head.

"I'm glad you told me about his disappearance. Let's keep checking the astral, and see what we can find. He told me about your vision. He worries about things more than he lets on. And I don't take visions or dreams lightly," he professed. "I think they can be warnings and we can take action to prevent them from happening."

She let out a deep sigh. "Thank you, Bryce. It helps having talked to you. I'm going to send myself back now."

"Before you go … While we've been sitting here talking, a long red gash has formed around your neck," he said frowning.

"Do you have a mirror handy?" she asked.

"Surprisingly, yes," he replied opening his desk drawer and handing it to her.

She cringed upon seeing her reflection. "How did this happen?"

"I don't know. It's been forming around your neck since you got here."

"This has to be related to Luke's disappearance. There is no logical reason why something like this would suddenly appear," she stated.

"Does it hurt?"

She gently rubbed her fingers over it, and said, "Yeah, it kind of does. I'll get to work on healing it. I should leave now. I'll be in touch."

He smiled and said, "You better."

Less than one minute later, she was gone. He looked out the window and saw that snow was lightly falling … *Big brother, where are you? I know deep down that you're in trouble. If you were dead, I'd feel it, and thankfully, I don't. We're going to find you. I should head home before this snow turns the roads into a traffic nightmare and Amber starts worrying. There's nothing I can do from here, anyway …* he thought, putting on his leather jacket and leaving the office.

He was correct in his urgency to leave and get on the road. The snow became heavier, and the roads worsened the closer he got to home. When he walked through the front door Amber threw herself into his arms and said, "Thank God you're home! We're supposed to get at least a foot of snow by morning."

Hugging her tight, he said, "I love coming home to you." He

continued holding her close and not letting go, remembering how he almost lost her two months earlier.

"What's wrong?" she asked sensing something was amiss because he was holding her a little too tightly.

"Luke's gone missing," he replied somberly, loosening his embrace and looking into her pretty blue eyes.

Her mouth dropped open and she asked, "He left her?"

"No, he didn't leave her; not willingly anyway. I'm sure he's been abducted."

"How? Who? Why?" She knew her voice sounded shrill, but the thought of someone abducting a hulking man like Luke was hard to envision. She helped Bryce out of his jacket and hung it on a hook by the front door. He took her hand and they sat down on the sofa in front of the warm and cozy fireplace, facing each other.

"What did she say?"

"She just showed up at the office," he replied taking a lock of her long, blond hair and wrapping it around his finger. "She can teleport."

Amber was speechless and stared at Bryce for a long moment.

"I had the same reaction, except Melinda and Ricky were sitting in my office and thankfully she appeared behind them, near the conference table and hid behind it. They asked if I had seen a ghost and I told them I just remembered I had to make an important call. My heart was pounding, I couldn't believe my eyes," he explained.

"How does she do it?"

"This will sound crazy, but she has a … magic rock," he replied.

"Seriously? What does it look like?" she asked.

"It looks like a plain old river rock with a tree carved into one side of it. She was distraught because Luke had a meeting with some construction guys at the new studio and was supposed to be home by 12:30, and never came back. He didn't call or answer his cell. She checked the astral and found his truck in the parking lot and the storefront locked up, no sign of him. She tried to find out more and was blocked by a wall. When she dissolved it she was surrounded by darkness and pushed back into her body. *Something's not right. I have a hunch that Elliott is behind it,"* he stated. "If he is, I'm concerned for her safety and what he might try to do to her."

"He's another psycho like Mike. And Mike is still out there, waiting to strike again. I was planning to fix a nice dinner tonight, but I've lost my appetite," she said collapsing against his chest. "I'm worried about Luke."

"So am I, sweetheart. I don't have much of an appetite either. You know Mike's still in Mexico. He's killed several more women who've spurned him, and every time I try to kill him, I'm thwarted. The universe has a mind of its own and all we can do is work with it. I'll never stop watching him though, and now I'll keep an eye on Elliott too," Bryce had some psychic abilities on the astral. He could influence someone's thoughts and do physical harm, even though he couldn't move objects with his mind. His emotional connection to Amber was so powerful that they sometimes communicated telepathically.

They remained close together on the sofa in silence, watching the flames burn high and lost in their thoughts of Luke. They were shocked by this unexpected turn of events and frightened for his life.

When Nina arrived back home, she found herself in the kitchen and took a seat at the table. Taking deep breaths she quieted her mind, held the rock and asked, "Please help me find him." The familiar warmth embraced her body, and a bouquet of red roses appeared on the table in front of her. They were surrounded by plastic with a packet of rose food wrapped inside of a rubber band around the gathered stems. Picking them up and inhaling their fragrance, she closed her eyes and received a vision of Luke following a clerk to a counter getting ready to pay for them when someone wearing a hooded coat came up behind him and Luke vanished. The tears falling down her cheeks tickled, and she wiped them away with her hand … *I would bet my life that Elliott is behind this. It's time I found out what he was doing.* She put the roses in a vase with water and then ventured to the astral.

Later that night when they finally succumbed to sleep, Bryce went to the astral determined to find his brother. Remembering what he mentioned to Nina about viewing Elliott's activities for the day, he took a look and confirmed his suspicions …

Nina joined him shortly thereafter and saw Elliott's treachery for the third time that evening.

"I had a feeling he was behind it," Bryce said after seeing Elliott stab the sword into Luke's back and watching him disappear. "That knife must be cursed. I've never seen anyone vanish into thin air from the touch of something. Where did he get an item like that?"

"He probably stole it," she sighed. "I saw the knife hanging on his wall and I had to touch it. As soon as I did, I received an image of an angry, medieval woman. The feeling was intense, so I snatched my hand away and left. It's not unusual for me to get impressions like that when touching an old item. However, every time I saw him after touching that old knife, the medieval woman would appear in my head and shout at me to stay away from him. Now the biggest question is, where did it send him? I've been trying for hours to locate him only to be met with one wall after another. I keep dissolving them and getting the same old darkness," she said.

"Have you tried looking into the knife's past?" he asked.

"Yes, and still nothing but walls and darkness!" she exclaimed.

"I gather you've already tried using the rock to help and got no-where, right?" he asked.

"I spent some time with it when I got home and saw what happened to Luke, but didn't see who stuck that knife in his back until I viewed Elliott's actions. Strangely enough, the roses appeared on my kitchen table. I've never encountered anything like this before. I've used every trick I know to break down barriers and fear he might be gone for good," she said. "We had so many great times together, and he's wonderful to be around. I truly love your brother, heart and soul."

"I know he feels the same about you. It's nice that you received the roses. You are all he talks about. I'm going to see if I can find him. Maybe since we're blood brothers, I'll have better luck or be able to grasp at something," he surmised.

"I sure hope so," she sighed.

Bryce proceeded to look for his brother and met with the same blocks and darkness that Nina had experienced. They tried looking for him together, thinking their combined love for him and strength of will might work better, only to be disappointed with the resulting darkness again.

"There has to be a way through this," Bryce said.

"I've tried using my thoughts to bore a hole through the darkness, and nothing," she replied.

"What about using a tool?" he asked and instantly created an astral drill.

"Try it," she encouraged.

Bryce used his astral drill and created a hole in the surrounding darkness.

"You did it!" she exclaimed and he peeked through it.

"Nothing but gray muck, I can't see anything," he said.

"I'm going to have to steal the knife from Elliott. I imagine he's probably got it hidden somewhere, but I'll find it," she stated. "If I have to stab myself to join Luke, I'll do it."

"Be careful, Nina. What if you do that and can't come back?" he warned.

"*I'll carry the magic rock in my pocket when I stab myself,*" she said.

"*What if the rock won't let you do it?*"

"*Then, I'll have to figure out something else.*"

"*I know I won't be able to talk you out of it,*" he sighed. "*If you can't bring him back, I won't give up on finding both of you.*"

"*You're a good man,*" she said smiling.

"*I'm going home now. Keep in touch, drop in if you need to,*" he said.

"*I will,*" she replied ...

Bryce glided back into his body and saw that Amber wasn't in bed. Figuring she was sleepwalking around the house, he went looking for her. She hadn't sleepwalked since being rescued from Mike's burning basement. He knew she was worried about Luke and that was enough to trigger an episode, especially since she had taken a sleeping pill before going to bed tonight. He checked the nearby bedroom that they had made into an art studio and found her sitting at her drawing board and sketching furiously. He hoped it was a clue to finding his brother.

Amber had an unusual talent for channeling information when she sleepwalked. She was an excellent artist and would draw pictures of things of which she had no prior knowledge. She never remembered anything upon awakening and was continually surprised and alarmed at seeing the things she drew during the night. He peered over her shoulder and saw her sketch of him and Nina surrounded by darkness and him peeking through a hole ... *It's starting again, she draws what I experience on the astral.* She flipped the page of her notebook and started to draw something different. He patiently watched her draw a picture of Nina lying dead with her throat cut, and Luke down on his knees crying ... *What is that about?* His thoughts strayed to the red ring he saw around Nina's neck.

CHAPTER 3

Hell's Hideaway

Luke awakened before Rogue greeted the day, and noticed that Nina's side of the bed was empty … *She's probably in the bathroom.* He thought how lonely it was to wake without her lovely, warm body pressed close to his. He glanced toward the bathroom and the door was open and the light turned off … *Maybe she's in the kitchen.* He listened for sounds, expecting to hear soft footsteps in the hall or faint noises from the kitchen … nothing. Something felt wrong. Getting out of bed, he walked toward the kitchen. It was empty and dark except for a nightlight near the stove. His apprehension grew stronger, the entire house was eerily silent … *I better find her asleep on the lounger.* Entering the sunroom he turned on the light and saw her lying on the chaise lounge, dead. Her throat was slit and blood pooled on the area rug and hardwood floor.

"No! This can't be happening, I'm dreaming!" he declared, rushing over to the lounger. Seeing her pale, lifeless body and vacant eyes staring up into nowhere was terrifying, and he convinced himself it had to be a lucid dream. "I know I'm dreaming, wake up!" he said to himself. Not being able to wake from what he thought was just a dream, he knelt down and touched her blood with the tip of his finger. He'd seen and touched enough blood in his life to know that this wasn't fake.

"This isn't real, this can't be real! Who did this to you?" he sobbed, and for the first time in his life felt completely, utterly helpless and traumatized. Tears rolled down his face, he could barely breathe, and his stomach indicated he was going to vomit. He forced himself not to spill his guts, and even though her cold, dead body was lying in front of him, it still didn't feel real. His emotional anguish and pain were acute, yet his mind kept telling him that this whole situation was wrong. Pinching and slapping himself hard, he tried desperately to awaken from this horrific nightmare. Something whispered to him in the back of his mind, something he should know, yet couldn't remember what it was. The one word which came to him was "snow." Even though it was still dark outside, he could see that there was no snow on the ground and no white flakes were falling from the sky. *I've got to call the police ...* Doing his best to remain rational, he began walking to the bedroom to get his phone when he heard pounding on the front door and a man's voice shouting, "POLICE, OPEN UP!"

Clad in just his boxer shorts, he opened the door to find three cops and four patrol cars with their lights flashing so bright he was momentarily blinded.

"I'm glad you're here, I was just going to ..." Luke wasn't able to finish his sentence before the officer interrupted and another one slapped handcuffs on him.

"Luke Decker, you're under arrest for the murder of Nina Perotti. You have the right to remain silent. Anything you say can and will be used against you in a court of law. You have the right to an attorney. If you cannot afford an attorney, one will be provided for you. Do you understand the rights I have just read to you?"

"Yes," he replied between gritted teeth, growing angrier by the second.

"With these rights in mind, do you wish to speak to me?"

"I DIDN'T KILL HER! I LOVE HER!" Luke yelled at the top of his lungs. "I'M ALMOST NAKED, BAREFOOT, AND IT'S FUCKING COLD OUT HERE!"

"You shouldn't have killed her then," the officer calmly replied as he and another officer led Luke to a patrol car.

He was losing control, something which was normally second nature to him and that he had cultivated throughout his life. He fought to hold his tongue as they guided him into the backseat of the police car ... *How do they know my name?* He observed that the officers were dressed in black from head to toe, wearing tall cowboy hats, cowboy boots, and each one was carrying and wearing their own personal arsenal of guns and ammunition. Once he was situated in the back seat, the officer pressed on the gas pedal and they went flying into an abyss. He lost consciousness due to the high rate of speed they were traveling.

Bugs were crawling on him when he woke up cold, shivering, and itching. The bug bites were turning into red welts along his torso, arms, and legs. Sweeping them away from his body, he stomped them to death with his bare feet. Most of the bugs were large and crunchy and oozed slime when he crushed them. The entire floor was crawling with insects, and he worked up a sweat in his mission to kill each and every one.

"It's a good thing I'm not afraid of bugs," he muttered, crushing the last batch. His feet itched and burned with the remains of bug guts stuck between his toes while he surveyed his surroundings with disgust. He was in a jail cell with a packed dirt floor beneath his feet and a toilet in the corner. Now that the irritating bugs were dead, his thoughts returned to Nina.

He missed her terribly and whispered with reverence, "Nina, I hope you can hear me wherever you are. I'm so sorry about this. I don't know who killed you. I don't know how they got past me in the night. But I will find them and avenge your death."

He heard heavy footsteps, labored breathing, and jangling keys heading in his direction. "I brought something for you to wear to your trial today," the gruff voiced jailer said. He was a short man with a beer belly hanging over his dark blue trousers. His matching blue shirt was at least two sizes too small and didn't completely cover his protruding stomach. He wore thick-soled black shoes and walked with a limp. He was balding with patches of grayish brown hair above his ears and wore black rimmed glasses. Taking his keys and opening Luke's cell door, he yelled, "Catch!" A dirty orange jumpsuit went flying, smacking Luke in the face.

"My trial is today? I don't even have a lawyer!" Luke snarled tossing the jumpsuit to the floor.

"You committed a crime and you're guilty. A jury will decide your punishment," the man replied, shrugging his narrow shoulders.

"I'm entitled to a lawyer, I'm allowed to make a phone call, and I didn't kill Nina!" he huffed with frustration.

"Not my problem," the man said shaking his head back and forth. "But, I'll see what I can do."

Luke watched him limp away humming a tune. Deciding a dirty jumpsuit was better than being practically naked, he struggled to put it on. It was four inches too short and didn't even come close to covering any of his muscular chest. He ripped off the sleeves to get his arms through the holes … *This is fucking ridiculous.* He was beyond the point of caring. The woman he loved had been murdered, and he was thrown in jail for a crime he didn't commit, not allowed to make a phone call or talk to a court-appointed attorney, couldn't recall the moment he lost consciousness before waking up in here covered in bugs, and nothing about this situation made sense. *If this is truly a bad dream and I wake up soon, I pray I never have another one like this.* Feelings of dread settled in his heart and he wondered if he would survive the day.

Roughly twenty minutes later, the potbellied jailer and three unusually tall cops, at least six feet six inches each, dressed in their finest head to toe black uniforms, arrived at his cell door.

"Hey, Decker, you can make your phone call now," Potbelly said holding out his hand.

"How'd you get my phone?" Luke asked.

Potbelly shrugged and said, "Either call or don't, it's up to you."

"What's the name of this jail?"

The three cops laughed loudly and Potbelly replied with a smirk, spelling out the letters: "J A I L."

Luke grabbed his phone from Potbelly and called Bryce. As luck would have it, he got his voice mail.

"This is Bryce Decker, please leave a message."

He didn't know what to say and held onto a shred of hope that this was all a dream. "Hey bro, it's me. I'm in jail, they think I killed Nina. I think I'm having a bad dream. This is not a joke. Please call me when you get this message. Thanks," he said feeling disappointed. He held onto his phone, not wanting to give it back; knowing that if Bryce did return his call, he probably wouldn't be informed of it.

"Time to go," one of the tall officers commanded, taking the phone away from him. Two others handcuffed him, shackled his legs, and led him out of the cell. Escorting him down long gray corridors, he noticed that each of the police officers were the same height and resembled one another in the face. This remained true when he entered the courtroom and the guards and the judge looked the same. The random people in the courtroom and the assembled jury, however, looked like the usual group. At least the judge had a nameplate, *The Honorable Abe Matthews*, the officers and Potbelly weren't wearing any name tags.

The judge knocked his gavel down and called out with authority, "Luke Decker, approach the stand."

This is odd ... he thought walking toward the judge, flanked by two officers.

"You're on trial for the murder of Nina Perotti. You slashed her throat when you caught her engaged in sexual intercourse with Elliott Greenwood. We have everything captured on video, and we will display to the jury and those assembled, your undeniable guilt," he commanded.

What the hell? She would never cheat, and certainly not with Elliott. She hates him. Is the government filming private things you do in your own home now...? Luke thought, when the lights dimmed and he watched the unthinkable. The screen showed Nina and Elliott making love in her bed. Luke walked in on them and pulled Elliott off of Nina, beating him unconscious and throwing him out the front door. Next, the video showed Nina crying and pleading for Luke's forgiveness, and him pretending to forgive her long enough to get her into a position where he could slash her throat.

He was nauseous after watching the video. Seeing her body entwined with Elliott's, the rapturous look on her face and enthusiastic participation, and the damning footage of him slitting her throat was painful to watch. His heart was breaking even though he knew it was a lie. He had to wake up, he was convinced that he was in the throes of a vicious nightmare, probably a dream within a dream ... *I'm going to wake up and Nina will be alive and loving me. Maybe I should try clicking my feet together. I'm not wearing ruby slippers, but here goes ...* he clicked his bare heels together in desperation, hoping to wake up or find himself home ... nothing ... *Am I in a coma? Do I have a brain tumor?*

Judge Matthews looked at the jury and said, "What's the verdict?"

"GUILTY!" the jury said in unison.

"Luke Decker, you are sentenced to death by guillotine. Your execution is scheduled for tomorrow morning at six a.m. Do you have any special requests for your last meal?" Judge Matthews asked.

"No," Luke replied, cold as a stone.

"Your last meal will be served at eight tonight. You can eat it, or not. NEXT," he roared.

The three cops escorted Luke back to his cell … *Perhaps if I die in this nightmare, I'll wake up in bed with Nina wrapped around me. If this isn't a dream then I'd rather be dead.* When he arrived back at his cell, bugs were crawling around in the dirt again. It appeared to him that they were placed there on purpose. Unable to stop thinking about Nina having sex with Elliott, he was stomping them to death and cussing like a sailor before Potbelly finished locking him in.

When Nina returned to her physical body, she was so distraught that she swallowed a sleeping pill. She rarely took any type of medication, but these capsules were a godsend tonight. Fifteen minutes later she was out like a light and dreaming about Luke …

> She is standing inside Luke's cell. He is sitting on a dirt floor with his head in his hands and a tray of half-eaten, cold food next to him. "Luke! I finally found you!" she says, rushing over to him, taking his hands in hers.
>
> He stares at her in bewilderment and touches her cheek. "Nina … what are you doing here, are you a ghost?"
>
> "No. I've been trying to find you on the astral. What is this place?"
>
> "I wish I knew, love. I'm in jail for allegedly killing you. I saw you dead, your throat was slit and I touched your blood. The police arrested me for your murder. I'm supposed to die tomorrow, by guillotine. This is some warped dream I can't escape from. I don't know what to believe … Did you have sex with Elliott?"
>
> "What? No, never! I swear to you that is the truth. Why would you think such a thing?" she asked.
>
> "They made me watch a video of you and Elliott having sex, and me killing you. I didn't believe it, but I wanted to be sure."
>
> "I've never cheated on you, I never will. I love you, Luke. I don't

want anyone else, ever," she swore.

"Sweetheart, you're fading, please don't go. Take me with you!" he panicked, gripping her hand as she gradually became transparent.

"I can't, something won't let me. I'll find my way back to you, I promise!" she cried and woke up in her bed, the warmth and feel of his hand lingering on hers ...

"*NO!*" she screamed, and succumbed to a fit of tears, punching her pillow over and over without mercy. "So close, I was so close. I've got to get back; they're going to kill him!" Objects went flying around the room while her anguish poured out. She continued her hysterical meltdown until exhaustion overtook her and she fell into a deep and dreamless slumber.

"Why didn't she take me with her? Was she real or my imagination?" Luke whispered in the darkness now that she was gone. Inhaling deeply, he could smell her scent; a refreshing honeysuckle fragrance she often sprayed in her hair. He didn't like feeling helpless and there was nothing he could do but hope that by dying tomorrow, he would be pushed back to reality as he once knew it.

He didn't recall falling asleep and awakened with a start when he heard Potbelly unlocking the cell, proclaiming, "It's a good day for justice. Time's up, Decker."

Potbelly was followed by the same three identical looking officers who escorted him yesterday. Luke got up from the floor taking his time and stretching. He wasn't afraid of dying, and hoped beyond measure that it would reunite him with Nina, wherever she might be. He stood still while they shackled him.

They walked in silence to an outside courtyard; the guillotine was straight ahead on a raised platform. A lively crowd was assembled and chanting repeatedly, "JUSTICE! JUSTICE!" Five other people were standing in line waiting for their beheading; three men and two women ... *I wonder if they're falsely accused too.* He was standing at the end of the line, a security gate banged closed behind him.

"What are you convicted of?" the young, skinny man standing in front of him asked, he couldn't have been more than twenty-five years old. He had curly brown hair, freckles, and soft blue eyes.

"Murder, but I didn't do it. She was ... is my woman," Luke replied.

"Same here. Only it wasn't my woman I was charged with killing, it was my sister, and I swear on the Holy Bible that I didn't do it," the man declared. "We were close; she was the only family I had left."

"I believe you. What is this crazy place?" Luke asked.

"I don't know. She was staying at my apartment because her boyfriend beat her up and threw her out. I woke up one morning, went into her room and found her dead. The police stormed my house and said I poisoned her; I was forced to watch their fabricated video showing how I did it. I hope this is a bad dream and once they chop off my head I'll wake up back home," he said with a heavy sigh.

"Me too. We're in the same boat, and right now it's sinking. Good luck to you, I hope you wake up in a better place," Luke said.

"Thanks, you too," he replied.

Their attention was diverted when Judge Matthews began to speak, sounding like an Evangelical preacher, "Good morning. Today we will see justice served for the poor souls we lost because of these six wretched murderers. Let them burn in Hell for eternity. Commence with the beheadings!"

One by one, each person stepped up to the guillotine to meet their fate, and the crowd cheered as each head rolled downhill and into a large container. The bodies were dragged away and thrown in a pile. Despite the many times Luke had looked death in the eye remaining calm and in control, this time he was petrified. He was sweating profusely, his heart beating rapidly because his gut was telling him that the worst was yet to come. His heart sank when he watched his new acquaintance lose his head ... *How did we get here? Maybe I really do have a brain tumor.* Now it was his turn. He walked to the guillotine and placed his head on the chopping block. Hearing the blade release, he closed his eyes to let death claim him.

Nina slept so deeply that she didn't hear Rogue welcome the dawn. She woke two hours later, cringing and wiping the sleep from her eyes and assessing the damage in the bedroom. Every picture had fallen to the floor, items from the dresser and vanity scattered across the room, the bedside clock had stopped working, closet doors were flung open and clothing was everywhere. Suddenly remembering her brief dream about Luke, sorrow and desperation rose to the surface and she dissolved into tears. It was times like this when she wished she could channel to find out if he was dead. Her psychic abilities didn't include being able to communicate with the departed, although she had never tried to do it. There wasn't anyone she was close to who had passed on that she wanted to contact ... *But if Luke is dead, I think I would be able to feel it.* A voice in the back of her mind said that he wasn't dead, so she had to believe it in order to get through the days ahead and formulate a plan to steal the sword from Elliott and rescue Luke.

I've got to get a grip. I created this mess last night, and now I have to clean it up. Before starting that daunting task, she put on her robe and slippers and walked through the house, checking to see how much damage she'd done during her breakdown. She chastised herself for losing her hard won self-control, and knew she must concentrate on maintaining her equilibrium while searching for Luke. The last time she had a meltdown like this was when she broke up with Jerry, other than being taken by surprise when Elliott and his goons broke into her house ... *Sometimes I hate my telekinesis.* The damage was confined to the bedroom. A few pictures had fallen off the walls, a lamp base was broken, and miscellaneous items overturned or strewn across the floor ... *Whew, I got lucky. At least I didn't start any fires this time.* Each of the fallen picture frames was intact and she hung them back on the wall.

Trudging into the kitchen, she noticed the coffee was ready and waiting ... *Thank God for automation, it should be potent after sitting on warm for two hours.* She poured a cup and sat at the kitchen table in silence, admiring the beautiful roses which had opened. Her heart was heavy with worry over Luke, and missing his cheerful morning presence that she had come to love so dearly. Mornings were their favorite time of day. She vowed to steal the cursed sword this afternoon and contemplated threatening Elliott with a painful death if he didn't hand it over. Her ire was rising, and she forced herself to calm down before she wrecked her home again.

After last night's heavy snowfall and the unplowed neighborhood roads, Bryce decided to stay home, and lingered at the kitchen table with Amber discussing her drawings and his astral adventure during the night; Luke's vanishing, Nina's roses, and failing to locate him.

"Wherever he is, I wish we could send Mike there!" she exclaimed. "Have you checked your phone yet?"

"No, but I will now," he replied checking the call log. "Well, I'll be ... Luke called!"

"*Play it,*" she pleaded, reaching out and taking his hand.

He set it on speaker and pressed play. She moved her chair closer to his. There was heavy static in the background and Luke's voice was so faint they could barely hear it. Bryce turned up the volume as loud as it would go and replayed the message. It was still faint, yet they heard his words, "Hey bro, it's me. I'm in jail, they think I killed

Nina. I think I'm having a bad dream. This is not a joke. Please call me when you get this message."

They looked at each other for a moment, both of them flabbergasted. Amber was the first to state the obvious, "He called you from another dimension. We couldn't make this stuff up if we tried."

Bryce nodded in agreement replying, "I'm going to call him back."

He dialed Luke's number, but it went straight to voicemail, "This is Luke, please leave a message." His voicemail greeting was audible, clear, and void of static.

"Bro, where are you? Nina and I have been searching the astral and were literally blocked from finding you. I don't understand your message. You haven't killed Nina. She's alive and worried sick over you, we all are. Call me as soon as you can. We love you, man," he stated, ending the call.

Amber let out a deep breath and said, "I hope he's still alive. We have to tell Nina."

Nina cleaned herself up and before putting her house back in order, she wanted to focus on slipping to the astral and stealing the sword. The housework could wait. Getting comfortable in her favorite chaise lounge, she concentrated on sending herself to Elliott's house ...

He was sitting on his reclining sofa with his feet propped up, watching TV and drinking whiskey. Glancing at the wall next to the entry door, she saw that the old sword was no longer displayed there; he was hiding it. "I should have expected this. He knows I can take things from the physical plane. Why is he drinking this early? It doesn't matter, he disgusts me." She received a mental image showing the sword was hidden underneath the seat cushions. "He's sitting on top of it ... how should I go about this? I'll create a disturbance."

He knew she would come for the sword, and was prepared to keep his butt fixed in the seat as long as he could stand it. He wanted to keep it close to him and hidden at the same time until he could get that magic rock; then he would stab her and send her to Hell. She thought of ringing the doorbell, however, with a foot of snow on the ground and no one living nearby, it would be obvious. Besides, his security cameras would show there was no one standing at the door.

"He has to get up to use the bathroom at some point. I'll just have to wait him out. He's going to be alert to any objects falling and it would be best if he thought I wasn't here," she groaned, not feeling patient enough to wait, knowing that was her best course of action. "If he carries the sword to the bathroom with him, he has to let go of it eventually." With great reluctance she hung out in his living room, watching a football game in which she had little interest.

She tried ignoring the sound of her telephone ringing; sometimes she could disregard it and remain in an altered state. This time her effort was futile, and she slipped back into her physical body …

"Hello, sis," Nina sighed, greeting Madison.

"Well, jeez, I thought you might be happy to hear from me. Since you've hooked up with Luke, we don't talk as often as we used to," Madison said, with disappointment in her voice.

"I'm sorry, Maddie … so much has happened, and none of it good.

"What's wrong?" she asked.

Nina told her everything.

"I'm so sorry. I agree, you've got to get that sword and work with the rock to save him. I know you can do it. I'll cast a protection spell for both of you starting tonight and continue it until you return with him safe and sound. Please let me know as soon as you get it," she pleaded.

"I will. I appreciate the spell too. So, what's happening in your life?" Nina asked.

"I had an amazing dream last night and wanted to tell you about it," Maddie began.

"I'm all ears."

"I dreamed I was having sex with a hot guy, except that I couldn't see his face. He was muscular and … well-endowed…"

"It's been a long time since you've been with a man, you're probably just horny," Nina retorted with a slight giggle, her mood lifting.

"When he wasn't kissing me, he kept calling me Cara, and telling me how much he loved me. Then I had the most wonderful orgasm, and unfortunately, woke up," she said. "It was so real that I could still feel his touch."

"I bet you can't wait to go back to bed tonight," Nina said.

"Yeah, but it probably won't ever happen again. It was weird how he called me by my middle name. Maybe because I like it better than my first," she pondered. "I hope I have more dreams of him making love to me. If this keeps up, I'll lose interest in looking for another man. He made me feel fantastic, and I can't stop thinking about him," she yearned. "It could be I'm going to meet him soon."

"Well, for your sake, I hope so. You've been lonely too long. There are still good men out there. Just don't fall for another Ryan, he treated you like crap," Nina warned.

"That's an understatement, and I've learned my lesson. If Luke has a worthy friend, let me know and I'll move to Charlottesville," she said.

"Actually, Luke has a friend who would be perfect for you. I've been meaning to tell you about him but I keep forgetting. His name is Noah Colton, and he's tall and muscular and unattached; a former Navy SEAL. He's funny and sweet. Luke hired him to be one of his instructors and he's been helping him with other things involving the new studio. He teaches firearms safety and loves spending time in the woods. He lives about thirty minutes from here, maybe he's the man in your dreams," Nina encouraged.

"Then I'll seriously consider moving there and meeting him," she stated.

"That would be wonderful," Nina replied. "You know I'd love it if you lived nearby."

"You know I'm looking to make a life change. Being a traveling photographer has gotten old. Sure, I loved the adventure once upon a time, but I want to do something else with my life," she said. Maddie was an award-winning wildlife photographer, but for the past three years hadn't traveled much. Instead, she had opened a photography studio near her home, turning down the expeditions that had previously excited her. She could talk to animals, and they were drawn to her, appearing from their hiding places and allowing her to photograph them.

"Well, the sooner the better," Nina remarked.

"I hope you find and save Luke *soon*. If I were going to handpick the perfect man for you, it would be Luke. I'm here for you, so feel free to call me anytime."

"Thank you, Maddie. I will," Nina replied. "I'm going to hang up now so I can steal that sword from Elliott. I won't rest until I get Luke back."

"Absolutely! Get going and call me when you have it. I want to hear your voice one more time before you go. In case you don't come back," she worried. "I'll give you three days and if I haven't heard from you by then, I'm coming to your house to make sure the animals are cared for."

"I appreciate that, but I'll be back soon and make sure I take the rock with me," Nina promised.

"You better! I'll talk to you soon, be careful."

"I will," Nina said ending the call.

Talking to Maddie helped lift her out of her gloom. She thought how nice it would be if Maddie moved to Charlottesville, fell in love with Noah and lived happily ever after. Knowing she had a sword to acquire, she shook off those fanciful thoughts and continued plotting how she would take it when her phone rang again.

"Hi Bryce," she said hoping he was calling to tell her news about Luke.

"How are you doing?" he asked.

"Hanging in there, plotting how to steal Elliott's sword. I went to his house this morning but he was sitting on it. It was underneath his seat cushion. I planned to wait him out because he would have to use the bathroom eventually. However, my sister called and I couldn't stay there, but it was good to talk to her. I was able to connect with Luke last night, through a dream. He was in a filthy jail cell and said he would be executed today for my murder. He said he found me dead, and that my throat was slit. I wanted to stay with him longer but something wouldn't let me, and I woke up in my bed and had a complete meltdown. I hope he's still alive, if he were dead I think I would feel it," she replied.

"I agree. I don't think he's dead either, not yet anyway. I wanted to tell you that we checked my phone and there was a voicemail from Luke. There was a bunch of static in the background and his voice was faint, but he said he was in jail for killing you and that he thought he was having a bad dream. He said it wasn't a joke and to call him back. He didn't say much else, but it's obvious that he's trapped in some hellish, alternate reality. Amber drew some pictures while she was sleepwalking last night, and sketched a picture of you with your throat slit and Luke on his knees crying. I think we are receiving *echoes* of things happening to him wherever he is, so I believe we will find him. All of us are still connected to him," he explained.

"That gives me hope that we'll be able to save him. Did you call him back?" she asked.

"Yes. I got his voicemail and assured him he didn't kill you, and that we have been searching the astral for him and are worried sick. I told him we loved him and to call me back. I doubt we'll hear from him, but I figured it couldn't hurt to let him know what was happening back here, just in case," he said. "It's amazing that he called from another dimension."

"We won't give up until we find him," she said. "I'm going to slip to Elliott's house and try to take the sword again. Thanks for the update. I'll do the same if anything significant happens, especially if I can get my hands on it," she emphasized.

"Okay, I'll let you go now. Take care," he said.

"You too. Bye." *I've got to have that sword. I'll check on the animals first and then go back.* On her way to the barn she stopped dead in her tracks *... That's it! Morgan is going to help me ...*

After tending to her own creatures, she appeared in Morgan's stable, and knew he would be instrumental in helping her. The beautiful Palomino recognized her astral form and greeted her by trying to nuzzle her head.

"Hello, handsome. It's good to see you, my sweet friend," she cooed gently stroking his white mane. "I'm going to clear a path for you so you can walk to the house and see Elliott." She continued talking to the horse for a few more moments and then focused on the deep snow. Placing her hand in her pocket and holding out the magic rock, she created a warm, golden light which melted a pathway into the heavy snow leading to Elliott's back door.

"Let's go see your owner," she whispered, and walked with Morgan to the back door. When they reached the back entrance she had to do something to incite Morgan to whinny and attract Elliott's attention. She conjured up two astral Rottweilers with a ferocious bark that only Morgan could hear. "I'm so sorry Morgan; I promise I'll make them vanish once Elliott comes to the door."

Elliott heard Morgan's frantic whinnying and jumped out of his chair. Throwing back the curtains he was surprised to see his horse in a state of panic. He opened the door and stepped outside into the cold

to calm him down. Morgan was frantic, finally turning and gallop-
ing back along the path to his stable. Elliott's mouth dropped open
when he saw the pathway through the snow. "THAT SNEAKY LITTLE
BITCH!!" he hollered.

Appearing in front of his sofa, Nina used her energy to throw the
seat cushions across the room. The sword was lying there and she fo-
cused on it with laser-like intensity. Feeling the tingling in her fingers
she knew it was time for action and took the sword. Now that she had
hold of it, she made the astral Rottweilers vanish and slipped back to
her home ...

Elliott hung his head in defeat. She knew Morgan was his sweet
spot and used him to get what she wanted. Elliott was bad to the bone,
although he treasured his horse and wanted to ensure he was okay.
Morgan was standing outside of the stable when he walked up to him.

"Hey, champ. It's okay. I don't know what she did, but it's alright
now and no one's going to hurt you," he said stroking his mane. "I'll
get even with her, I promise."

⚜

After he finished comforting Morgan, he walked back into his
house and collapsed on the sofa. It was time to create a servitor to take
back his sword. Even though he hadn't created one in over two years,
he was confident he could do it again. He was outraged that she had
gotten the best of him and his heart was filled with malice. Knowing
he had to calm himself to properly create the servitor, he concentrated
on his breathing until he was able to focus his intent. The first step was
deciding what the servitor would look like, what it would be named,
and its appearance should be tied to its functionality. It was clear to
him that it should have multiple limbs and move lightning fast to have
a better chance of taking the sword and trapping Nina. He decided to

create a gigantic black octopus and call it Octo. Staring at the white wall in front of him, he used his mind to build and project the image. He made sure it looked formidable and was larger than life. To make it look especially creepy, he gave it a human face. The face had black hair, red eyes and a frightening mouth with shark-like teeth.

Three hours later, he finished creating its physical form and it became real. He chanted Octo's name over and over, thinking of the evil he wanted to unleash upon Nina—until it came alive. He knew he was rushing this, as it usually took him two days or more to fully charge and empower a servitor, but there was no time to waste. Octo might not last as long as he wanted, however, it would get the job done, and if he needed to recharge Octo later, so be it.

"Octo, take back my sword from Nina Perotti," he commanded. "This is what she looks like and this is where she lives," he said showing Octo pictures of her and her home. "Stab her with the sword and bring it back to me, today. Go!"

"I'm on my way," Octo replied, leaving the house.

Elliott wanted Nina sent to Hell, and he would break into her house and find the magic rock after she was gone. Feeling mentally and physically drained from creating Octo, he sank down into his chair and slept.

CHAPTER 4

Troubles Aplenty

Luke woke up lying flat on his back on a deserted beach. His parched and aching throat hurt so badly that it burned; his body was wet and cold. Before he could think much further on his present condition, a wave crashed onto the shore drenching him with water and he choked. Rolling over onto his side, he spat out the foul-tasting sea. Struggling to his feet, he saw that he was still wearing the ill-fitting orange jumpsuit. Once his eyes were able to focus, he looked up and saw a dreary, overcast sky. *I didn't die after all. I don't know if that's good or bad. At least my head's still attached.* He walked along the beach noticing that everything was various shades of black and gray; gray sand, black sea, and gray sky ... *I'm living in a black and white photograph.* The wind picked up, chilling him to the bone. There wasn't a soul in sight, and the beach seemed to go on forever. He kept walking until he saw a cloaked, hooded figure in the distance and thought it was the Grim Reaper. All he could see was a hooded and robed body without a face moving toward him ... *Maybe death's finally coming for me.*

As the figure came closer, he saw there was still no face to this hooded entity. When it stopped directly in front of him, he moved to the side to continue walking and the figure moved with him, blocking his path. It was tall, standing approximately six feet five inches.

"Who or what are you?" Luke asked trying to hide his growing anxiety at facing what he thought was walking death. He hated the raspy, gravelly sound of his voice and wished he could have something to drink.

It laughed at him and a deep masculine voice from the void said, "They call me DK."

"Alright, DK, are you human?" Luke asked, continuing to stare into darkness where there should have been a face, hoping he hadn't offended the strange being. He thought it was odd that this creature spoke with a British accent.

"Do I look human?" DK asked, placing his black-gloved hands on his hips.

"No, I'm just trying to figure out *what* you are and why you don't have a face," Luke said feeling more curious than afraid. He observed that DK's gloved hands were not skinny or skeletal.

"That's none of your business!" DK thundered.

Luke began coughing uncontrollably and thought this might be the end as his throat was so dry he was coughing up blood. He fell to his knees on the sand while his body heaved. When he could stand it no longer, DK reached out and put a large steel canteen in front of his face.

"Drink!" he commanded.

Grabbing the canteen, Luke drank his fill. The water was cold and soothing as it slid down his throat. He finished the canteen, breathing a sigh of relief when the coughing finally ceased.

"Thank you," Luke said peering up at him. "What is this place?"

"A special place in hell is reserved for your enemies, and this is that place," he replied.

"I have no shortage of enemies," Luke responded looking down at the gray sand. "Can you tell me who sent me here?"

"Take a wild guess," DK growled.

Luke closed his eyes and saw Elliott's face. "Elliott Greenwood."

"Ding, ding, ding! It didn't take you long to figure that one out," DK taunted laughing.

"*How* did he send me here?" Luke asked.

"That's not for you to know," DK declared.

"Are you the one in charge?"

"Perhaps."

"Can you help me get home?"

"No."

"You showed me kindness by giving me water. Why?"

"I never show kindness. I'm simply keeping you alive for future torment."

"Is this eternal or am I going to die here?"

"You are stuck here until your earthly time is up, so the answer is yes. However, most have died before their time, all of them suicides. No one has ever escaped from here."

DK was gone before Luke had time to blink. He wanted to ask more questions about this hell hole. His throat no longer plagued him and other than being cold through to his bones, he felt okay. He continued walking along the desolate beach thinking about the mysterious DK, and wished he could remember the exact moment before he woke up and found Nina dead. He remembered the dream he had about her and hoped she was still alive … *I was once a Navy SEAL and the training was brutal. Whatever befalls me here I have to pretend is part of that training, otherwise, I'll lose my mind.* With thoughts of Nina and her magic rock, he wished that she would find her way here soon and take him home. The sound of a motorboat drew his attention and he looked to the ocean. Sure enough, a boat was speeding in his direction and he told himself this was another test. He stopped and waited until they dropped anchor and came ashore. He knew they were coming for him and trying to escape would be pointless, better to face this and get it over with.

Three rough-looking men got out of the boat. Two of them were his height, muscular with short, buzzed haircuts and non-descript faces. The taller one was a long-haired redhead with a scruffy beard, nose ring, and tattoos down his exposed, muscled arms. They were menacing, sloshing through the water the rest of the way to the beach. One of the buzz-cut guys was carrying a large sack over his shoulder. "Hey, Decker, it's payback time," the red-bearded giant shouted.

"Payback for what?" Luke asked.

"Let me refresh your memory," Redbeard said punching him so hard in the stomach that he fell on his knees and hurled. "That was for my best friend, George Tomkins. Dead by your hand, you son-of-a-bitch!"

Luke looked up, trying to catch his breath and replied, "George was an abusive bastard who raped his sister and drowned her dog in the river."

When Luke got out of the Navy, he went to work for the CIA and spent time with a team of assassins. He was a tracker who told them where to find their kills. Finding and killing bad guys didn't bother him in the least. In his mind, he truly believed he was helping to rid the world of worthless filth. Several years later, he worked on other underworld missions and never lost touch with his former team. They eventually became freelancers and he joined their hitman business for the private sector, on the side. They didn't indiscriminately accept money to kill people. Luke was the first point of contact for someone looking for a hired gun, and he performed due diligence on the intended target before passing the information to the actual shooter. Sometimes he enlisted Nina's help for verification with difficult cases, but he liked the sleuthing. It was a complicated web. On more than one occasion he became incensed when learning the truth of an intended target and asked for the assignment. He used the money he made from these kills by donating it to abused women's shelters, animal rescue organizations, and children's charities. In one or two isolated cases, he did it for free. These past few years he had distanced himself from the hitman business because most of the hit people were becoming too greedy and accepting anything just for the money. He occasionally referred someone to them, but that was as far as it went. His days as an avenging angel were over.

"You didn't have any proof!" Redbeard shouted.

"Oh, but I did, and George deserved what he got," Luke snarled, remembering the shy and broken victim who sought his service. He didn't charge her a penny. He felt that a bullet was too good for George and made him suffer instead.

"Bullshit. Now it's time for you to meet the same fate," Redbeard stated. "Roy, Jake, put him in the sack!"

Luke attempted to fight off these brutes, inflicting some serious pain on them. However, they were big and strong like him, and he was outnumbered. They handcuffed him, stuffed him in the sack, carried him to the boat and tossed him in. Luke gave up struggling because each time he moved someone punched him … *Drown me and get it over with.* They took their time riding away from the shore hoping it would prolong his agony. Luke prepared himself for drowning and used mental tricks to avoid panicking. Part of him hoped he would die and be done with it. Roughly twenty minutes later, they stopped the boat and tied a heavy weight around the sack.

"Overboard!" Redbeard ordered and the three of them threw Luke into the sea.

Roughly two more minutes before I drown and wake up in another hell, according to DK, or maybe I'll really die this time … he closed his eyes feeling his body rapidly descending into the ocean, and pictured Nina's beautiful face in his mind waiting for the inevitable.

"I did it! This sword is mine and I'm going to find Luke," Nina declared after entering her body. The sickness which usually plagued her whenever she took something from the astral sent her running to the bathroom. She wouldn't let go of the sword, keeping a firm grip on it while she retched into the toilet ... *I hate this!* When her stomach finally settled, she flushed the toilet, let go of the sword for a few moments to wash her hands, gargled with mouthwash and walked back to the sunroom. Relaxing in the lounger, she knew that a migraine headache would soon follow and fully expected to be sick the entire day. Picking up the phone, she texted Maddie and Bryce letting them know that she had possession of the sword. Maddie texted back words of concern, wishing her luck and telling her to be careful, and Bryce did the same. Maddie repeated her promise of hightailing it to Charlottesville if she didn't hear from Nina in three days.

Gripping the sword's handle, she felt flush with warmth even though her house was cold. She became dizzy and the room started spinning ... *Oh God, what's happening?* It wasn't long before the spinning ceased, and a thick fog appeared, taking a while to clear. When it did she believed she had traveled through time ...

> *She is standing inside a modest, thatched dwelling, watching the beautiful woman with long, black curly hair applying salve and bandaging an injured man's well-muscled arm. A fire burns brightly in the hearth, and assorted pots of herbs line an adjacent table. Nina gasps in astonishment when she realizes that she knows this woman and the man with her, and that she is viewing events in 13th century Scotland. "OH MY GOD ... NO!"*
>
> *"Thank ye again, Sorcha. Yer a fine healer, the verra best. I dunna*

know how this village, or me, would survive without ye," the big, bare chested man wearing a kilt says to her. His hair is long and blond, falling well past his shoulders, and his eyes are blue. He is a handsome and powerful looking man in this time, and known in the 21st century as Elliott Greenwood.

"Yer most welcome, my laird," she replies giving him a sweet smile as she finishes bandaging his arm. Nina can't believe what she's seeing or the startling recognition that she was Sorcha in a past life.

"Callum. Ye must call me Callum when we are alone together," he replies, reaching out to touch her cheek.

"Aye, Callum."

"Stay with me tonight. My guard will escort ye to my chambers and see ye safely home, as always" he says.

She places her hands on her hips and says sharply, "I willna be yer mistress forever. Marry me or be on yer way!"

"Ye know I canna marry ye, lass, even though I want to. Should I ever choose to marry, it must be to a noblewoman. Marriages are for clan alliances, not love. But, my heart would only belong to ye," he replies, pulling her onto his lap.

"Callum, I willna share ye with another woman," she states pushing away from him.

"There is no other woman," he says pulling her back to him.

"Not yet, but there will be. Ye are the new laird, ye must have a wife to give ye heirs," she says.

"Aye, 'tis true. Although, ye could be carrying my bairn right now," he replies placing his hand on her stomach.

"Tis not possible. Ye know that I know what plants to use to prevent catching a bairn. If I were to have yer bairn, he or she would be a bastard and never allowed to rule this clan," she says.

"And ye know I would claim any child of mine. Aye, they willna be able to rule, but they will be cared for and loved," he replies.

"And what of yer wife? No noblewoman would be kind to their husband's bastard children," she claimed.

"Dinna fash yerself ... I am not married yet," he says with a smile and kisses her passionately. "I want ye now, I canna wait until tonight. Ye know I love ye."

Nina sees him pick up Sorcha, carry her over to her bed and make love to her. Nina attempts to move forward in time because she doesn't want to watch them have sex. However, when she tries to move forward, it doesn't work. She is forced to watch. "I have to admit that Callum/ Elliott was smoking hot. All muscled and strong; poor Sorcha, poor me! I'm glad I never bedded him in my present lifetime." As she watches them make love, she sees other images of the two of them having secret trysts, Sorcha sneaking into the castle under guard to spend nights in his chamber. Nina sees that he rarely went to his bed without a willing woman next to him. Sorcha was his favorite, but she wasn't his one and only.

Time moves forward by several weeks, and the village is excited and talking about the recent announcement that their new laird is betrothed to the eldest daughter of a neighboring laird whose lands border Callum's. Sorcha is heartbroken, even though she knew this day would come. Nina sees Sorcha and Callum arguing when he comes to her home and attempts to seduce her.

"Go away, unless ye need healing," Sorcha tells him when she opens her door. "Ye will be married soon and I told ye, I willna be yer mistress!"

"But ye are the only one who holds my heart. I love ye," Callum replies, forcing his way into her home while his two guards remain outside.

"We are done, my laird. Go back to the castle and be with yer betrothed," she states. "I willna share yer bed with another woman!"

"But ye have been sharing my bed with others," he says with a smile. "Ye are the one I love; the others are just for fun."

Sorcha is hurt even more by this new information and turns her back on him. "Get out, leave this moment!" she demands.

He grabs her and spins her around to face him. "I am Laird, and I will have ye whenever I wish, I own ye, and don't ye forget it! If ye refuse me, I will throw ye in the dungeon!"

He stomps out of her cottage, slamming the door behind him. Sorcha breaks down in tears and cries out her emotional pain. A few hours later she stands in front of the blazing fire in her hearth and chants a spell of protection to keep him away. Nina sees that the spell is effective and Callum doesn't darken her door in the coming weeks. Sorcha repeats this spell once a week so it will remain a strong deterrent. During this time, she meets another man who helps her forget Callum.

It is early morning when she hears a knock on her door and opens it to find four men standing there with looks of panic on their faces. She recognizes them from the village. Two of them are carrying a large man named Magnus, who works with the metalsmith and is unconscious. His leg is wrapped with pieces of torn fabric, drenched in blood. The men had stopped the bleeding as best they could, but he was weak from losing so much blood.

"Sorcha, we need yer help. We were hunting and Magnus was attacked by a wolf!" Angus exclaims as Sorcha opens the door wider and lets them inside. "Do ye think ye can save him, lass?"

"I will try, lay him on the table here and I will see what I can do," she replies and the men lay him down on top of it. Sorcha carefully peels away the fabric and proceeds to clean and disinfect the wound. "Out with all of ye, I need room to work and save yer friend. If I can keep the wound from becoming infected and he doesn't die in fever, he might live," she claims and shoos the men out the door.

"Thank ye, lass," Angus says as she closes the door.

Sorcha tends to Magnus, and he stays at her cottage for seven days until he is strong enough to go home. They get to know each other during this time and she wonders why she never noticed him before. He's taller than Callum, and while not as thick with muscles, he's a strong and fine-looking man, and deeply grateful to her for saving his life. His reddish gold hair falls to his shoulders and his brown eyes are soft with kindness. Nina recognizes this man as her beloved Luke.

On the morning he is well enough to leave, he asks Sorcha to marry him. "Thank ye for saving my life. I've fallen in love with ye, and would like to ask if ye will be my wife?"

Sorcha throws her arms around his neck and he pulls her close for their first kiss. "Aye, I would love to be yer wife!" she states with a squeal of delight.

"We will marry today. Father Logan is my cousin, and he will be verra happy to join us," Magnus says and kisses her again.

"That would be wonderful, and this will be yer new home!"

"Aye, and we will never be apart."

Sorcha and Magnus walk to the church and are married a few hours later. Nina sees in the weeks which follow that Callum is furious with her for marrying another man. Now that his new bride is pregnant, he continues to take willing women to his bed each night and ignore his wife. He's wanted to visit Sorcha, yet every time he is near her cottage, he is overcome with stomach pains and heart palpitations. "She's more than a healer, she's a witch," he grumbles to himself one evening while thinking how to get her alone. He continues dwelling on it and devises a plan.

Meanwhile, Sorcha and Magnus are blissfully happy together and on their one month anniversary as husband and wife, he gives her a special gift.

"My sweet wife, I made something just for ye. I know ye can protect yerself with yer spells, but I would feel better knowing ye have this when I'm not here," Magnus proclaims and places the simple sword he made for her into her hands.

"Thank ye, husband! I shall cherish it," she gushes, kissing him. "It is perfect. The scrollwork on the handle and the red stone hilt are lovely."

"Aye, and if ye look closely, ye can see our initials within," he replies, pointing it out to her.

"Ye hid them verra well!" she remarks.

"I wanted ye to know that this sword belongs to ye. Many have requested similar swords with scrollwork. Tis a lovely design and I thought ye'd like it."

"I love ye, Magnus mine," she says.

"I love ye too," he replies.

While watching the story of Sorcha and Magnus, Nina has observed that she hasn't reinforced her protection spell since she married him. Nina gets a feeling of where this is headed and fears the outcome will be disastrous.

Callum has been spying on Magnus and knows that he goes hunting every morning before starting work in the metal shop. He knows what he's going to do. He makes sure that Magnus is gone before he pays a visit to Sorcha. He disguises himself as a commoner and slips past his guards through a secret passageway. When he knocks on her door, he no longer feels sick to his stomach and his heart beats normally.

Sorcha opens the door, looks at her visitor and doesn't have time to scream before he rushes inside, bolts the door, and throws her on the bed.

"Get off of me!" she screams pushing against his chest.

"Sorcha, it has been too long. I hunger for ye, and I will have ye!" he growls and pins her body with his weight. She continues to struggle against him and kicks him in the groin with her knee.

He falls off of her onto the floor, clutching his groin and groaning in pain, "Ye witch, ye will regret this!"

She moves off of the bed and runs past him when he grabs her ankle and trips her. She falls to the floor, hitting her head and losing consciousness.

He slowly rises to his feet and spies her sword on the table next to the potted herbs. Smiling to himself, he takes her sword and hobbles out of her cottage. Even though his groin is aching, he continues walking slowly toward the woods. After a short time, he spots Magnus with his bow and arrows. Magnus stops and looks around as Callum hides behind a nearby tree. Magnus begins walking again and Callum throws the sword, stabbing him in the back. Magnus falls to the ground and dies shortly thereafter. Callum makes haste back to the castle and slips in unnoticed through the secret entrance.

A few hours later, Sorcha is aroused from her unconsciousness when Angus and Hamish burst through her door, carrying her dead husband. Her head is aching and when she sees them carrying her lifeless Magnus, she falls apart.

"MAGNUS! NAY!" she wails as the two men lay him face down on the table so she can see the sword sticking out of his back.

"I am so sorry, lass. When we came upon him in the woods, it was too late," Hamish says softly as a tear falls down his cheek.

"The laird did it! He came in here and tried to rape me. We fought and I must have hit my head when he tripped me. He stole my sword and killed my Magnus!" she cried.

"Och, Sorcha, ye canna fight the MacNeal. Ye will end up in his dungeon, or worse," Angus stated. "We are so verra sorry for yer loss … it is our loss too. He was my best friend."

Sorcha is beside herself with grief and slumps over his dead body, crying her eyes out.

"Please leave, I wanna be alone," she requests.

"Ye know where to find us, lass. Ye dunna have to go through this alone. We will help bury him," Hamish says and they leave her alone with Magnus's body.

"I canna live without ye, Magnus. I dunna want to live without ye. I love ye too much!" she sobs so hard her whole body shivers. "He killed ye with my sword, and I will avenge yer death!"

She pulls the knife out of his back and cleans off the blood.

"*Magnus mine, I'll love ye forever. Ye were a good man, too good for this.*" *Her tears stop flowing and her anger rises.* "*I willna be long for this world, but before I go, I will send Laird Callum MacNeal to hell!*"

Getting up, she stokes the fire until it's raging. Taking the knife and holding it out in front of her, she stands close to the hearth, feverishly chanting a curse in Gaelic. Sorcha spells this knife for vengeance against one's enemies. Whoever stabs their enemy with this knife will send them to a hellish dimension where they will suffer every wrong they've ever done to another, any dark violence wished upon them, and bring their deepest fears to life. They will know misery and great suffering. They will remain in this otherworldly hell until the end of their earthly life—because death is the only way out. She further empowers it to help one track down their enemy wherever they might be, and to reward the owner with intuitive insight.

Nina feels the overpowering strength of Sorcha's emotional energy which, combined with her words, casts a powerful spell. Although she doesn't speak Sorcha's language, she knows exactly what she is proclaiming with her spell, and is astonished to learn that her psychic abilities have been with her in more than one life.

When she is finished with her spell, she places the sword under her pillow and collapses onto the bed. She is sweaty, exhausted, and drained of energy. With her husband's dead body growing cold on the table, she falls into a deep sleep until Callum rushes through her door, jarring her awake.

He bolts it shut and without saying a word strides over to her bed. She quickly reaches for the sword but he knocks it out of her hand before she has a chance to stab him.

He pins her to the bed in a way that prevents her from kneeing him in the groin again, and chokes the life out of her.

Nina is distraught because Luke is the victim of her ancient spell and the bad guy has gotten away again …

"I'm so sorry Luke. It's all my fault!" She sobs with her head in her hand, and her heart feeling like lead in her chest ... *What a horrible spell to put on something. I was a monster. Wouldn't just vengeance be enough? How many people have suffered because of me?* Overwhelmed with anguish, and thinking of the hurt and pain people endured through the centuries because of her spell, she seriously considers jumping off of a cliff. Her head ached with the anticipated migraine, and at this moment she felt she deserved it. Sick from misery and exhaustion, she closed her eyes and slipped into a light sleep.

An hour later, she awoke to a cold and quiet room, her right hand still clutching the sword. Putting her left hand in the pocket of her cardigan, she was relieved to feel the magic rock still there. Closing her hand around it, she let its comforting warmth embrace her. Her headache began to lessen and was gone in a matter of minutes ... *I need to feed my animals and make sure they have enough food to last for a week or more* ... With that thought in mind, she stood up and slipped the sword underneath the seat cushion. She didn't like leaving it out of her sight, yet knew that she had to see to her creatures and needed both of her hands free. She slipped into her snow boots, grabbed her coat from a peg near the door and headed outside. The sun was fading and it would be dark soon. Outside the air was cold and sharp, and the wind was picking up. She ran through the deep snow to the barn, leaving an ample supply of food for her goats and chickens. Next, she ran to Buttercup's stable to ensure she had enough to eat. She left the stable open so Buttercup could roam the property and wouldn't be cooped up.

Gently stroking Buttercup's mane, she said, "I'll be back as soon as I can sweetheart. I left the door open so you can wander, just in case I'm gone longer than planned, and you have plenty of food and water. I love you girl, and watch out for Patches."

She heard a meow when her calico cat rubbed against her legs. Bending down to pick her up she said, "Patches, sweetie, I have to go away for a little while, but you've got enough food, and Buttercup will keep you company. If I'm not back in three days, Maddie will take care of you." She kissed her on the head and set her back down. Patches and Buttercup were an unlikely pair, but they enjoyed each other's company and she usually found them hanging out together. Buttercup allowed Patches to sit on her back, and Nina laughed whenever she saw her cat riding her horse. Satisfied that her animals were provided for, she ran back to her house before dusk settled in.

Once inside she took off her coat and boots, put on her slippers and walked into the sunroom, reclaiming the sword from underneath the seat cushion. She screamed when she noticed the enormous black octopus with a hideous human face standing in the corner of the room, it was terrifying. Two pictures fell off of the wall and it moved through the air toward her, its arms never touching the ground. She was familiar with servitors and knew this was Elliott's creation come to do her harm and take back the sword. She gripped it tighter.

"What does he want?" she asked.

"He wants his sword back," Octo replied.

Before she could blink, Octo wrapped one of his arms around her waist and lifted her into the air. "Give me the sword," he demanded, squeezing her so tight she could hardly breathe and using one of his other arms to try and wrest the sword from her grip.

"If you don't let me down, I'm going to stab you with it and send you to Hell!" she threatened.

"I can squeeze you to death and that's exactly what I'm going to do. You can either surrender the sword to me or die," he sneered.

Knowing she wouldn't be able to help Luke if she was dead, she relented and said, "Here, take it."

Octo took the sword from her and lessened his grip, but did not let her go. "I have orders to send you to Hell," he said.

"Go ahead, I was going to send myself there anyway," she replied knowing the rock would keep her safe.

Using his other arm, he stabbed her in the chest with the dagger and she vanished.

"That was too easy. She didn't even put up a fight." He was sorely disappointed that she hadn't fought him.

Octo returned to Elliott's house carrying the sword. Elliott was ecstatic to have his weapon back.

"Did you stab her and send her to Hell?" he asked, excited that his plans were becoming a reality.

"Yes. She vanished upon impact," Octo confirmed.

"Did she put up a fight?"

"No. She said she wanted to go there; although I can't imagine why."

"Excellent! Your job is finished, thank you," he said clapping his hands together. "You can hand it back to me now."

"What if I don't want to?" Octo asked. He liked the sword and thought it was a grand prize.

"You must. I command you to hand the sword over to me!" Elliott demanded, glaring at Octo and beginning to think he had made a mistake bringing him to life.

"No. I'm going to keep it." Octo defied him.

"Why, what use would you have for something like that?" Elliott asked, annoyed with his creation.

"I like it, that's reason enough. You like to steal things which don't belong to you, why can't I?"

He hated that Octo was right. The monster he created was much like him. He didn't want to admit that when he brought Octo to life, he was thinking and feeling evil, selfish, and negative thoughts which became part of Octo's personality. Alarm bells were ringing in his head and he replied, "Because you are nothing more than a tool. You forget that I created you, and I can also make you disappear."

"You're an asshole and I don't like you," Octo replied thrusting the sword into Elliott's stomach before he could respond.

Elliott disappeared just like Nina did, and Octo felt victorious. "This thing is really useful. I'll go have some fun with it."

CHAPTER 5

Wicked Ways

Lily Nolan had seen much of the world; however, her favorite place to be was walking alone along a white, sandy beach with clear blue water. She preferred solitude when she wasn't seducing men, taking their lives and energy to remain young and beautiful. She was alarmed when she looked in the mirror this morning and saw that she had aged at least twenty years overnight. Her tight abdomen had become flabby, and her generous breasts were sagging. Her shiny, dark brown hair was showing some gray, and laugh lines were deepening around her mouth. She was still a gorgeous woman and intended to stay that way, no matter how many men must be sacrificed. It had been exactly two weeks since she'd been with a man. She was growing tired of the endless sex she must have to remain immortal and beautiful.

For several years, she had been regretting the deal she made with the Devil so long ago. She vowed to get back on track and knew she must work her magic on her looks immediately, in order to attract the sexiest and most virile man she could find, her peace of mind depended on it.

An hour later, she was dressed in a tiny thong bikini, her figure tight and shapely. Her long hair flowed down to her waist without a trace of gray. She was ready to set a man's desire to flaming. Setting her beach tote and blanket on the sand and donning her sunglasses, she tossed aside her flip-flops and strolled, slow and sexy, along the edge of the water, putting out the vibe that she was ready for action.

Mike Collins had been enjoying his time on the Mexican Riviera, safe from the law out to arrest him back in America. He let his hair grow back some, having previously shaved his head, and fled the country wearing a sandy colored toupee and colored contacts. He knew his naturally curly dark hair would make him easily identifiable so he bleached it and wore it in a buzz cut. He went by the name of Hector Torres. The ocean calmed his nerves, helped him forget about Amber, and proved to be the perfect place for dumping his victim's bodies. He had met plenty of available and willing women, yet once they got to know him they tried to flee and none of them made it. Sitting on the sand and watching scantily clad females walk by, he noticed her … *What a perfect body; I could do her all day and night.* He stood and walked toward her, glad he was wearing tight-fitting trunks and had kept up his weightlifting routine.

Lily watched him moving toward her. He wasn't as tall as she preferred her men, but he was taller than her by a few inches, and had a smoking hot body. Nicely muscled with a dark tan, spiky, short bleached hair and brown eyes, he would do just fine. Her eyes strayed to his snug fitting swim trunks and she licked her lips. She smiled when he came closer and introduced herself.

"Hi, I'm Lily," she said extending her hand. Looking into his dark eyes, she could see his past and knew he was just as evil as she; this was going to work exceptionally well. Their climaxes would be legendary and provide exactly what she needed.

Taking her hand, he brought it to his lips for a kiss. "It's nice to meet you, Lily. You have a pretty name which suits you perfectly. I'm Hector."

"Would you like to walk with me?" she asked taking off her

sunglasses so he could see her luminous gray eyes. She knew his name wasn't really Hector, but she went along with it.

"Yes, I'd walk with you anywhere," he replied still holding her hand. They walked in companionable silence to where she had left her beach towel and tote; both were growing highly aroused and ready to get down to business.

"Why don't we find a more secluded area and get to know each other better?" she asked sweetly, picking up her towel.

"I agree. It looks like if we walk further that way, we'll have more privacy," he replied excited at the prospect of doing it out in the open.

"Let's go," she responded and he picked up her tote and grabbed her hand. They walked away from the crowd and found a spot of sand where they could explore each other without anyone gawking at them.

He helped her lay down her towel and noticed two more inside her beach bag. He took one and spread it out next to hers. They were lying close to each other, enjoying the feel of the sun when she turned toward him and cupped his groin.

"I want you, Hector," she purred. "I think you want me too."

"Can't you tell?" he replied turning to face her.

"Put it inside me, please," she breathed.

"Gladly!" he exclaimed slipping off her thong bottom while she quickly divested him of his trunks. "Let's use this extra towel to cover our lower bodies," he suggested as he positioned himself on top and entered her.

"You feel so fine," she said, capturing his mouth in a deep kiss. They writhed together for several moments before exploding in a soaring climax. He saw stars and flashes of light before he blacked out, she was ravenous and wanting more ... *Two more times and I can take his essence.*

He regained consciousness ten minutes later and was still inside of her. "Come again," she whispered and began moving her hips, bringing him back to life.

"You've cast a spell on me," he said feeling rejuvenated and pounding into her again.

"Yes, I did," she sighed, urging him on.

Their second coming was even fiercer than the first. This time he blacked out for some time, and when he woke up, she was gone. He heard laughter and saw her frolicking in the waves and a boat sitting on the sand which he hadn't noticed before.

She waved and called to him, "Hector, let's go for a boat ride!"

He pulled on his trunks and walked over to her. He should have been exhausted after two sessions, but he was hungry for more. His desire had increased tenfold, and he wanted to spend the rest of the day pounding away inside her.

"Where did you get this? I don't know of any boats for rent around here," he replied taken aback and feeling cautious, despite his growing lust for her.

She placed her hands on her hips and replied, "You were out for at least half an hour. I have friends around here. I asked to rent a boat, and they brought one to me."

He couldn't take his eyes off of her delectable body and was satisfied with her answer. "Well then, let's go for a ride," he said.

"We can rock it," she suggested with a gleam in her eye.

"I would like that," he replied, amazed that he was ready to do her again. He had never felt this kind of lust.

"I can tell," she said winking at him.

They swiftly moved the boat further into the water, jumped in, started the engine and sped away from the shore. He was content to let her drive the boat. He sat close beside her, roaming his hands all over her body.

"You're the most desirable woman I've ever met," he breathed. "I want you so badly, more than the first and second times. When do you want to stop?"

"How about now? We're out far enough and no one's around," she replied gently squeezing his cock. Will you drop the anchor?"

"Certainly," he replied.

She took off her bikini and was ready for him once the anchor landed. He dropped his trunks a second later and sat next to her. She climbed on his lap and began riding him. Wrapped around each other they rocked to a screaming, earth shattering climax. They remained joined together, draped around each other in a relaxed state of total bliss. She lessened her hold and pushed away from him to look in his eyes. Once he gazed into those steely gray orbs he was powerless to look elsewhere.

It didn't take him long to figure out that he was completely paralyzed and unable to move. To his utter horror, the beautiful, sexy woman who just gave him the greatest carnal pleasure of his life morphed into a revolting, ugly old woman with scraggly white hair, loose wrinkled skin, and rotted teeth. Giving him a wicked smile she plunged her gnarled hand into his chest. He screamed in agony as she yanked out his heart and ate it in haste. Using dark magic, she made sure he was still alive and completely lucid, yet unable to move or speak. Laughing at his distress and becoming young and beautiful once again, she dove into the sea and swam several feet away. While treading water, she faced toward the boat looking directly at him. He watched her inhale deeply, and upon her mighty exhale the boat burst into flames.

She let out a delighted shriek, and in the blink of an eye transported back to her spot on the sand ... *He was delicious, what a perfect day! I could go for another one, although I don't need to do anything for a month. I'm just going to relax and enjoy the sun.* Bad guys were so much more fulfilling than the good ones, and she focused on them exclusively, unless it was an emergency situation, then she would take what she could get. Not every man succumbed to her charms, which is why she had to join with them three times before she could take their lives. She hated that rule and there was nothing she could do about it. Most of the really bad guys were physically abusive and she was used them taking their pleasure once and discarding her. And then there were bad guys who wouldn't give her a second glance. The day was too nice to dwell on those depressing issues. Instead, she laid back, closed her eyes and dreamed of the one man she loved and could never have. Despite the fact that she blamed him for putting her in this situation, she still carried a torch for him.

⁂

Bryce awakened in the middle of the night and discovered that Amber wasn't lying next to him. He knew she must have fallen asleep in her studio and probably drew something in her sleepwalking state. He walked down the hall and there she was, fast asleep with her head lying on top of her drawing board and colored pencils scattered on the floor. She sleepwalked almost every time she took a sleeping pill, and was deeply worried about Luke. He picked up the fallen pencils, placing them back in their case.

"Hey beautiful, wake up," he said bending over her sleeping form and kissing her cheek.

"I did it again," she yawned through a sleepy haze.

"At least you don't go very far," he kidded and she leaned into him, resting her head on his chest. He glanced at her newest drawing and his jaw dropped.

"What on earth?"

Rubbing her eyes and looking down at her new sketch of Mike naked with his heart ripped out and being eaten by an old hag, she said, "Oh my ... That is really gruesome!"

Knowing that she usually drew more than one picture during an episode, she flipped back a page and they both inhaled at the detailed, erotic drawing of Mike and a beautiful dark-haired woman having sex in a boat.

"I think you should check the astral, he's likely dead by now, I hope," she said. "He got what he deserved although it frightens me to think that demons really exist."

Squeezing her tight he replied, "I hope it's true, and then we can stop worrying about him coming back for you. She obviously seduced him first and then ripped out his heart. An evil succubus did us a favor, although he didn't deserve any pleasure before his death."

"Let's go back to bed. I can rest easy knowing that he no longer roams the earth," she said.

"We don't know that for sure. I'm going to check the astral ASAP," he replied taking her hand and walking down the hall to their bed-room. "I need to try and reach Luke again."

"What if Mike's not dead?" she asked.

"Then I'll have to keep watching him," he answered.

Getting back into bed, they curled up together and she fell asleep. Excited at the prospect of proving that Mike was dead, he found it challenging to concentrate on leaving his body. An hour later he was relaxed enough to seek his proof . . .

He watched in awe while the female demon seduced Mike three times before yanking out his heart and destroying him in a fiery explo-sion. "Now that was the icing on the cake. He got what he deserved for leaving Amber tied up to die in a burning house. Good job Karma. Thank you!"

He tried again to find Luke and found himself surrounded by thick, gray fog.

"Luke, where are you?" he called out.

"Your search is pointless. Give up and go home," a deep, booming voice replied.

"Show your face," Bryce demanded.

"As you wish," the voice answered.

A tall, dark-cloaked figure emerged from the fog and Bryce was face to no-face with a hooded figure.

"Are you holding my brother captive?" he asked, fascinated because this grim reaper had no face. He had dealt successfully with dark entities before and was unafraid of this one.

The reaper shook its faceless, hooded head at Bryce in a gesture of no.

"Then who is?"

"You know who sent him here and that is all you need to know," the voice answered.

"Who are you?"

"They call me DK, and you had best be on your way. Leave now and I won't have to kick you out. Believe me, you will be hurting once you return to your body!"

"You don't scare me," Bryce retorted and then wished he could take back his words ...

Returning to his body with a jolt, and wincing at the sharp pain in his lower back and legs, he attempted to get out of bed ... *Lesson learned, you're not invincible and DK shouldn't be messed with.* Amber was still sleeping when he hobbled into the bathroom and filled the deep bathtub with nearly hot water, turned on the massaging jets, and slowly sank down into it hoping to find some relief.

The atrocious stench of mold, urine, and feces assaulted Luke's senses as he slowly regained consciousness with a breathy inhale. It took a few moments for his disorientation to pass and his breathing to normalize ... *It seems I didn't drown.* He was surrounded by total darkness and the sounds of people in pain and anguish. He was facing a stone wall and his arms were stretched wide, his wrists and feet were bound in chains to that same wall ... *I'm naked. They're going to whip me.*

This was in Nina's vision and just might be my undoing ... closing his eyes he fought to remain calm. He knew it was going to hurt something terrible; however, he had trained his mind to withstand a great deal of pain. He heard the cell door creaking open, the sound of footsteps and a whip cracking against the floor. It was time for another payback. Images of a past life ran through his mind, of a time when he was the proud executioner for a powerful king. One of the many people he put to death was a palace insider who was spying for the king's enemies. This spy's capture and death helped to avert a vicious and deadly uprising. He knew that the soul inhabiting the spy's body in that place and time was Elliott.

Elliott couldn't believe his good luck. Although his own creation had turned against him and sent him to Hell, he was thrilled to be controlling this situation and live out his revenge fantasies against his enemies. This was his chance for payback to Luke for doing the same to him in a past life.

"Luke Decker, funny meeting you here," Elliott's voice was drenched with contempt. He was elated that he had landed in a position to inflict pain upon his enemy. Placing the torch he was carrying into a sconce on the stone wall, he cracked his whip onto the floor.

"I know why you're here," Luke said.

"You could apologize and maybe I will go easy on you," Elliott jeered.

"No you won't. You will derive great pleasure from torturing me. And for the record, I am not sorry for killing your miserable ass. I doubt you've ever lived an honorable life," he disparaged.

"Speak for yourself, you're no better than I am," Elliott belittled him.

Luke didn't respond because he knew there was truth in Elliott's words. He couldn't recall his other past lives and knew he had done many unsavory things in his current one. To his credit though, his intentions were good and his goal had been to bring justice to the wicked. He regretted the methods he employed to reach that goal and thought that he was just as bad as those he sought to destroy. He wasn't a religious man, although he said a silent prayer asking forgiveness for his sins ... *Dear God in Heaven, I am truly sorry for the bad things I've done in this life. I see now that the road to hell is paved with good intentions. Please forgive me for the pain and suffering I caused others, and if it is your will for me to die today, I humbly accept my fate. I ask one thing before I leave this world, please take care of Nina and keep her safe from harm. She is the best thing that ever happened to me, and thank you for bringing her into my life.*

"What? No response? I figured as much!" Elliott spat cracking his whip against Luke's back. He winced from the pain, bracing for more.

"Did you know that we used to fool around?" he taunted. "I've seen the butterfly tattoo on her right butt cheek. She has a *sweeeeet* little bottom!" Elliott snapped the whip again, this time striking him across his buttocks.

Luke didn't answer. He was sure that Elliott was lying and trying to get a rise out of him, though he remembered Nina telling him that she had feelings for Elliott from time to time. A seed of doubt was planted and he wasn't certain what to believe. He recalled the many photos she had hanging on the wall of her with different men. Granted, there were plenty of group photographs of her with other friends from rock climbing, white water rafting, skydiving and other outdoor adventures. She took the lovers' photos down the day they agreed to become a couple. He understood why she kept photos of previous conquests; it was a way of insulating her heart against involvement. Nonetheless, he wanted to know how Elliott knew about her butterfly tattoo, and he preferred to hear it from her. Luke loved staring at it when they did it doggy-style, and the thought of her doing the same with Elliott made his blood boil. Still, he kept his cool. He tried convincing himself that whatever she did before they made a commitment to each other wasn't important. After all, he hadn't been a saint either, and couldn't blame her for seeking pleasure when he had nothing to offer at the time.

"Cat got your tongue?" Elliott asked.

"I have nothing to say to you," he responded through clenched teeth.

"That's because you know I speak the truth," Elliott said cracking the whip two more times across his back, in the same place.

"No. I don't believe you for a second," he replied.

Elliott was enraged by his lack of response. Wanting him to seethe with jealousy and fight back, he continued ripping Luke's skin to shreds.

CHAPTER 6

Past and Present Collide

Nina unexpectedly found herself in a large room surrounded by hundreds of small screens, each one showing a different movie. Remembering the rock, she put her hand into the pocket of her sweater and was glad that she still had it. Concentrating on the different movies playing on the screens, she observed that the room was unnervingly silent and, in each movie, someone was suffering or being punished. Her first thought was of finding Luke. She was overwhelmed with frustration because she couldn't find him right away.

"Luke, where are you?" she whispered, searching the different screens for signs of her beloved. Turning to get a better look at her surroundings, she jumped and screamed when she saw the imposing figure of the Grim Reaper standing in a corner. Even though it had no face, she could feel it watching her. Thankfully her hand was inside her pocket and wrapped around the rock giving her the strength to look away from it.

"Who are you?" she asked staring down at her feet, afraid to look at it for fear it would grab her and escort her straight to Hell.

She looks exactly like Mother ... and those eyes, I know those eyes. She's so pretty, I can't believe she's really here ... "They call me DK," his deep voice boomed.

She continued staring at her feet, terrified of looking at him and thinking it was odd that he spoke with a British accent. Long moments of silence weighed heavy in the room and she turned her gaze back to the endless array of screens depicting shocking torture, she kept searching for Luke.

"Humanity is its own worst enemy. It has been this way since the dawn of time. Such a waste of human potential, not to mention the destruction mankind brings to the natural world. I really have to wonder what God was thinking when he created us," DK professed. "If I were God, I would have done things differently."

"Where is he?" she asked, her voice quivering.

She fears me, and rightly so. I rather enjoy her discomfort. It's not every day I get to antagonize my baby sister ... DK laughed loudly at his thoughts, something he hadn't done since landing in this dimension.

"Why are you laughing? This isn't funny!" she said with indignation and a bit of fear.

"I'm laughing because I frighten you," he replied ... *Such a fiery little thing.*

"Please take me to Luke," she begged still searching the screens.

"And what are you going to do when you find him?"

"Save him."

DK laughed again. "I wish you luck with your endeavor, my dear," his voice dripping with sarcasm. "Look at me."

"Why?"

"Because, right above my head, ten screens up and the fourth screen to the right, you will see him."

Nina looks up and sees Luke severely beaten by Elliott, who continues tearing him to shreds. "Luke, I'm coming and I'm going to take you home!" Whipping out the magic rock, she holds it up, commanding, "Take me to him!" She no longer cares that DK is watching her; she has to save Luke.

She has my rock! DK watches in amazement when he sees the twinkling particles rise from the rock, encircle Nina, and she disappears. He decides to follow her because he wants his rock back. He knew the rock was his when he saw the tree carved on it. In this dimension, he had superpowers and enhanced vision. Memories of a long ago, but never forgotten – time and place penetrate his defenses, and the tears start falling ...

He was five years old when his world fell to pieces. From his secret hiding place, he watched men in bizarre clothing and frightening weapons kill his parents. They had been expecting a hostile takeover from foreign invaders, yet were overly confident in their planned defenses and were taken by surprise. He knew his baby sister, Risella, was hidden in the private nursery along with his Aunt Yamora, or Mori as she liked to be called. Still reeling from the shock of seeing his parents die, he knew he had to save himself, his sister, his aunt, and anyone else who was still alive; there would be time for crying later. Using hidden passageways, his father showed him and where he often played, he ran as fast as his little feet would take him until he reached the nursery.

Mori was pacing nervously back and forth while Risella slept peacefully. Her head jerked around when she heard the door open. "Tendaris! What has happened?" she huffed.

"Mother and father are dead. They invaded the castle and are killing everybody," he said choking back the tears.

"I was afraid that would happen. I told my brother over and over that he was too confident and we should have left before they got here!" she spouted and then opened her arms. "My sweet boy. You know what must be done to ensure our survival," she said and he ran into her embrace. "I will raise you two as my own, far away from here. We must leave quickly, without being captured." This was devastating for him and he clung to her, crying his heart out. "You must be brave. We have to go now," she stated, pushing him away. "I have something to give you

which will keep you safe and well. I only have one of these and it is very special."

Reaching into her dress pocket, she pulled out a rock with the image of a tree carved into one side. "These are rare and precious and will help you navigate through life. They were abundant on this planet in ancient times, until a greedy king demanded they be mined for his use alone. Once the king's men mined every last one of them, they were kept in his private vault for a long, long, time until the palace caught fire and all of them were destroyed. Your great-grandfather had a few of these and gave one to your father and to me. I don't know where your father kept his hidden, but he carved the tree onto this one for me when I was just a few years older than you," she said handing the rock to him. "I only have one, so keep it protected and share it with your sister. If anything ever happens to me, I want you to use this rock to remain safe. It works with your energy, and with practice, you can do amazing things and have anything you desire." She was feeling extreme resentment toward her brother for not using the powers of his rock to defeat the invaders before they gained a stronghold, and now it was too late.

His tears stopped falling and he looked at her thoughtful. "Has it given you everything you want?"

"Yes. I've been happy and blessed, until today," she answered.

"But it didn't bring back Mindar. You were sad when he died last year."

"It cannot bring people back from the dead. It might help them come back if they are on the brink of death, but not after they are already dead. If that were so, I would bring back your parents right now. This rock helped me overcome my grief. I believe that in time, I will find another man to love," she said.

"I will take good care of it. I promise," he said placing it in his coat pocket.

She was like a second mother to him. Looking into her golden brown eyes, so much like his father's, he felt like he still had a part of him. She wore her light brown hair long and flowing, and his father had done the same.

"I know you will. Now, let us get out of here," she said, situating Risella in the crook of her arm and grabbing Tendaris's hand. They hurried down another hidden passageway which led to a secret chamber.

She knew exactly where to place her hand upon the gray stone wall to let Daneda know she was there. A portal opened and Mori entered the chamber with her niece and nephew. Dani was deeply sad and lamented, "I truly wish this day had never come. We were warned, and it could have been prevented. Now, we must trust in the hands of fate."

"You know we have to leave this planet, you too Dani," Mori stated.

"What is an old woman going to do on another planet?" she sighed.

"You're not an old woman! You're a wise and beautiful elder, and with your magic, you can do anything," Mori countered.

"Our magic does not always work on other planets. No matter, we have to leave and the star gate will only be open for a short while. I cannot hold it open much longer. Tell me, where do you want to go? Planet Earth is remote enough that no one will ever find us. They are human, like us, and we will blend in easily."

"Earth? Are you insane? It is so far away. They are barbaric, warring people and no better than the savages who invaded and are destroying our planet. It wouldn't surprise me if the invaders are from Earth!" she shrieked. "Please, I beg of you, do not send us to that backward place. What about Pondoria?"

"We know the Pondorians are human, but people without red hair are treated like citizens of the lowest class, especially aliens from another planet. Even if we had red hair, I wouldn't agree to go. All true Pondorians know each other, and they will know we are aliens. Life will be hard for us there," Dani responded, shaking her head.

"What about Elgon?"

"My dear, they are worse than Earthlings. They never evolved. All women are slaves and used solely for pleasure and child bearing. If you cannot bear children or have reached the end of your child bearing years, they kill you," she answered.

"What about Varling?"

"No! They are only partly human and filthy, nasty creatures. We would be better off with the Pondorians."

"What makes Earth any better?"

"Earth is an unusual place. We can choose which era to live in. We can go backward or forward in time. They are much less evolved than us, this is true. However, many countries there are very tolerant and anything goes. Men marry men, women marry women, and women can become men and the reverse. You can wear whatever you want, live with anyone you want, and no one cares. We need to make a decision and fast!" she urged.

"How do you know about these other planets?" Tendaris asked.

"We have scouts who travel to these other worlds and report their findings," she replied.

"Let's go to Earth," Tendaris said.

"I guess so," Mori replied, feeling defeated and hopeless. "We don't have any good options at this point."

"What time should we travel to?" Dani asked.

"The current era, and to a country which is open and tolerant of foreigners."

"We will go to America," Dani decided, and they walked with her to the portal. She entered a long sequence of numbers and symbols into a brightly lit panel at the star gate. A few moments later, the portal opened into a black void.

"I'm scared," Tendaris said trembling.

"It will be okay, you'll see," Dani soothed, taking his small hand in hers. Mori clasped his other hand and hugged Risella to her.

The four of them stepped into the void together. Unknown to them, someone had tampered with the star gate and they were immediately

*separated from each other. This frightened Tendaris and he reached
into his pocket to grab hold of the rock. He made the mistake of taking
it out of his pocket and accidentally dropped it somewhere along the
way. Tendaris and Risella landed on planet Earth, each in a different
place and time. Mori and Dani did not …*

Arriving in Luke's cell, Nina screams at the top of her lungs,
"*STOP!*" Luke is unconscious and bloodied so badly that she thinks he is
dead. His body hangs limply from his shackles and chains and his blood
is dripping onto the floor.

Laughing, Elliott turns to her and says, "Too late, sweetheart. He's
dead."

In a fit of fury, she throws her rock at him, striking him hard on the
forehead, and they both vanish. DK catches the magic rock before it
lands on the floor. He doesn't want it to break or chip from impact so
he slips it into his pocket. Releasing Luke from his handcuffs and shackles, he places him over his shoulder. Once he gets Luke positioned, he
takes out the rock and places it on Luke's destroyed flesh, saying, "Stay
alive a little longer. I promise I will get you out of here." Surrounded
by twinkling dust particles they are transported to a forest.

Nina is standing in between two great horses dressed in medieval
clothing. A rough and barbaric looking man with long brown hair and
a scruffy beard, wearing a kilt and dirty tunic, hands her an enormous
claymore sword. It is almost as big as she. Its total length is sixty inches
with a blade of approximately forty-five inches.

"Lass, use this sword and one of my horses to take your vengeance,"
he said. "Let me help you onto the black horse, and then I will strap
the sword to your back."

Taking her by the waist, he picks her up and settles her onto the giant horse. Her long skirts are in the way and she lifts them up, situating herself astride the animal. The man peruses her bare legs with interest, his blue eyes sparkling as he mounts his own horse and moves closer to her.

"What is your name?" she asked.

"Angus," he replied, and she allows him to strap the claymore to her back, helping to flatten her long and curly unbound hair. "When you see him, all you have to do is take the hilt with both hands and strike him down."

"Thank you," she said reaching over and touching his arm.

"My pleasure, lass. Go north and into the woods, you will find him there. Good luck to you," he said, trotting off in the opposite direction.

Spurring her horse forward they rode like the wind.

Something tasted like dirt and grass. Waking up face down on the ground, Elliott's tongue was lolling against the forest floor. Slowly rising to his feet and surveying his surroundings, he observed that it was extremely quiet. There was a chill in the air and he was cold. He was shocked to discover that he was wearing just a kilt and some strange looking boots. He couldn't help noticing that his legs, chest, and arms were thick with muscle, and his hair was long. Hearing the faint thunder of a horse in the distance, he took off running for his life. In a flash, he knew who was chasing him and the heinous crime he committed centuries ago, one of many back then ... *But that was another time and I was the laird! I had every right to say who lived or died.* He ran for what seemed like an eternity, and becoming severely winded was forced to slow down to a fast walk while his heart boomed in his chest and he struggled to breathe. The sound of hooves and a woman screaming grew closer and he couldn't muster the energy to continue running.

She was furious. Bloodlust and adrenalin flowed through her veins and she pushed her horse to the limit. Yelling a continuous string of Gaelic curses, her heart was pounding the closer she came to her target. She burst through the trees, a wild woman with long black hair billowing behind her, gripping the enormous sword with both hands. He wasn't surprised seeing her face, and the murderous rage in her golden brown eyes. Nina had come for him. He tried to flee except that his feet were rooted in place and he was unable to move. Thrusting her sword down upon him so hard that she split him in two, she cried, "THIS IS FOR LUKE AND MAGNUS!" His last thought before he died was that she looked exceedingly beautiful with long hair. His earthly time was up.

After cutting him down, she raised her bloody sword into the air with a shout of victory. Suddenly her horse reared up throwing her to the ground, knocking her unconscious and breaking her neck.

DK had his hands full. Luke was slung over his shoulder, soaking his cloak with blood and near death when he picked up Nina, carefully placing her over his opposite shoulder. He had to work fast because both of them were about to die and he couldn't lose her again, not when he had just found her. He knew they were at exit points in their lives. Exit points are openings where souls can decide to leave their current life or continue living until their final expiration date. Most souls build a few exit points into their life path in the event that something happens that is too overwhelming for them, so they have the option to leave early. It is a decision that is made at soul level. Adding to his urgency was the fact that the overlords could stop him at any moment and end his miserable life. Carrying the rock in his pocket gave him a measure of protection, but he wasn't sure how long it would last and felt that he had waited too long already. He wanted to let Nina have her revenge, and now it was time to make a run for it and get out of here.

Reaching into the pocket of his robe for the rock and feeling the comforting warmth spread through his body, he held it up to the sky and said, "Take us to a safe haven." In his mind's eye was the image of Luke's brother.

CHAPTER 7

Homecoming

Bryce and Amber were naked beneath the sheets, holding each other and basking in a state of post-coital bliss, when they heard a loud thump and crash coming from downstairs.

"What was that?" Bryce huffed. They jumped out of bed throwing on their robes. Slipping his handgun into its deep pockets, he said, "Stay behind me, honey."

She nodded her head in agreement.

Stepping quietly down the spiral staircase, both were wondering how anyone could have gotten into their heavily secured home. When they saw what awaited them in the living room, they picked up their pace and raced down the remaining stairs.

The coffee table was overturned, and Luke and a woman with long black hair were sprawled unconscious on the floor. Kneeling over them was an incredibly tall man with light brown hair to his shoulders, checking for signs of life. Luke was lying face down and naked with ugly, bloody lacerations and shredded skin covering his entire backside, head to feet. His blood pooled onto the hardwood floor. The woman was lying on her back, her neck twisted at an unnatural angle, unresponsive and deathly pale. She was dressed in medieval clothing.

Moving closer they saw it was Nina, and she was taller than the last time they had seen her.

"Who are you?" Bryce demanded, pointing his gun at the intruder. He was shocked and terrified thinking that they were dead.

"I'm David Kellaway, and I'm not going to let them die," the tall man replied and opened his palm which was holding the magic rock. Closing his eyes, he envisioned them whole and healthy, and chanted a prayer in Latin ...

Gazing directly into the sunny, distant light should have been blinding, yet it warmed their exhausted souls and was growing brighter. Luke clutched her hand and said, "This wasn't how I planned it. We were supposed to spend the rest of our lives together and then reunite on the other side. I was looking forward to our journey."

"But this feels so good, doesn't it? We're truly going home. And, we can ask to be together again in a new life to finish what we started," she replied, smiling and reaching out her other hand toward the ever-increasing light.

"Yes, it does feel wonderful. Although, I have too many regrets from our old life. I regret that I didn't fall in love with you sooner, and realize how happy you make me. I regret many of the things I did for the Agency. I'd like to start fresh and leave the dark karma behind. In our next life, why don't we be simple farmers and live off of the land?"

Laughing, she replies, "It doesn't matter to me, as long as we're together."

"The light is beckoning us. I'm going to ask those in charge if we can have some time alone before we come back again," he said.

"A honeymoon in Heaven, that sounds lovely," she agreed, embracing him. "Let's go into the light as one," she said.

Holding her close, he replied, "Forever as one."

Bryce and Amber watched in wonder when the rock released its twinkling fairy dust surrounding Nina and Luke's bodies. Luke's mutilated backside began healing, the skin sewing itself back together until he looked good as new. His blood disappeared from the hardwood floor. A blinding flash of white light encompassed Nina, illuminating the already bright room and causing them to turn their heads away. When it cleared they saw the color returning to her face, her long hair gone, she was wearing jeans, a black shirt and slippers, and a red cardigan. She was no longer a few inches taller. Both of them appeared to be sleeping. Bryce smiled when Amber ran to the couch grabbing a folded blanket lying on a seat cushion and covered Luke's bare bottom with it.

"It might be a few minutes before they regain consciousness. Nice place you have here," David said. Though he looked threatening with his towering height, long hair, large frame and wearing a long, black hooded cloak which hung to the floor, his green eyes were filled with warmth. Bryce and Amber were speechless and processing the miracle they had just witnessed.

Seeing them barefoot in robes late in the morning he smirked and said, "I hope you two had a chance to finish before we barged in."

"Yes, we did. And it was a glorious prelude to seeing my brother and Nina safe and sound," Bryce answered with a wide grin, extending his hand. "Thank you, David. I'm Bryce, and the beautiful blond is my fiancée, Amber. I'm forever in your debt. Please, have a seat and let us bring you something to drink." The two men shook hands and then David extended his hand to Amber.

"You are truly an angel," she beamed shaking his hand. "What can I get you to drink? Wine, beer, soda, water, coffee? Are you hungry?"

"A glass of water would be wonderful, thank you," David replied. "It's chilly in here, do you mind if I start a fire?"

"Be my guest. They will be nice and warm when they awaken," Bryce said pointing to the small stack of firewood next to the hearth. David picked up several logs and placed them in the fireplace. Instead of striking a match, he pulled the rock out of his pocket, held it in his hand and focused on the logs. In less than thirty seconds a blazing fire was warming up the house.

"Are you a wizard?" Amber asked walking back into the living room with a glass of water in her hand.

"Of sorts, thank you," David replied taking the glass from her and swallowing. "This is good."

The sound of their voices caused Luke to stir and awaken. Discovering he was naked, he pulled the blanket around to his front and slowly sat up. Seeing Nina lying on her back, he leaned over to kiss her cheek and whispered in her ear, "Nina, sweetheart, wake up. We're home."

She emerged from her slumber looking into the eyes of the man she loved, "You're alive!" she cried throwing her arms around his neck.

"Yes, and I'm delighted to see you," he answered hugging her close.

"How did we get back? The last thing I remember was slicing Elliott in half and falling off my horse," she said.

"You cut Elliott in two?!" Luke asked in disbelief.

"She did, and she was magnificent!" David pronounced. They both looked up from the floor to see a six-foot five-inch man with green eyes in a black robe smiling down at them.

He laughed at the surprised looks on their faces and said, "They call me DK."

Bryce erupted in laughter and said, "I should kick your ass for booting me from the astral like you did! I still have a sore rump."

"I was just doing my job," David replied, shrugging his shoulders. "By the way, I quit. They can take that job and shove it. My proper name is David Kellaway, and I'm pleased to meet you," he said with a bow.

"What happened?" Luke asked, feeling confused, happy, and loaded with questions. He couldn't understand why he was in Bryce's living room, Nina apparently killed Elliott from on top of a horse, and DK was human. The last thing he remembered was Elliott shredding him with a whip, and hearing a distant female voice screaming.

"The short version is that Nina stole Elliott's knife, put my magic rock in her pocket and sent herself to the dark realm," David began.

"Not exactly. Elliott created a servitor who came to take the knife back and he's the one who stabbed me. He was a giant black Octopus," Nina corrected.

"We searched the astral and couldn't find you," Bryce chimed in.

"She arrived at the entrance to our realm and I was sent to greet her," David explained. "I showed her where to find you, Luke, and she took out that rock and sent herself there. I followed her because the rock belongs to me and I wanted it back."

"Elliott was whipping you and told me you were dead. I hurled the rock at him and we both landed in another dimension where I killed him. I must have fallen off of my horse because everything went dark and I woke up here," she recalled.

"The horse threw you and broke your neck, Nina. I already had Luke slung over one shoulder, and I picked you up and placed you over my opposite shoulder. Then I asked the rock to take us to a safe haven. The first thing which popped into my head was a mental image of you, Bryce. And it all worked out, even if we did interrupt your interlude with Amber," David grinned.

"I don't know what to say except thank you. Nina and David, you have my deepest gratitude. I want to repay you somehow," Luke said feeling humbled. "David, who or what sent you to that dark dimension?"

"An evil woman whose affections I would not return," he replied.

"Were you stabbed with the sword?" Amber asked.

"Yes. She tricked me and I landed in that hell," he said.

"But you were a guard for that dimension. How did you become one?" Nina asked.

"My charm and persuasion, naturally," he quipped and was met with a few laughs. "Seriously, it's true. For what seemed like an extremely long time, I was subject to horrible karma like everyone else. I was an English knight and a warrior before I was sent there. I had seen many battles and accrued a good share of bad karma, including residual karma from past lives. I kept calling for the ruling overlords to show themselves, begging and pleading with them to let me be a part of their realm. I was willing to do anything to get the torture to stop. When they finally showed themselves I made them an offer. I would become one of them and act as a guard for the dimension. I boasted of my talents and experience, and why I would be a perfect guard. They scoffed at first and said that they weren't in need of any more guards. They refused my request and disappeared. However, a few hours later, they reappeared and said that one of their guards turned against them and that they would allow me into their league. It happened at a good time, because my torturer had just shut me inside of an Iron Maiden."

"What is that?" Amber asked.

"A wicked and painful torture device. It is a standing coffin with spikes on the inside. It has double-doors which open in the front and a place for the victim to stand. There are strategically placed spikes inside each door. Once those doors are shut, the spikes pierce vital organs. The spikes are short, so the wounds aren't instantly fatal. The victim gradually bleeds to death, slowly and painfully. The most horrific thing about it is that two spikes are deliberately positioned to penetrate the eyes. So, you can see why I was willing to do anything to get the pain to stop," he said.

"Ouch! Did they take away your face once you became a guard?" Luke asked.

"They didn't do anything to my actual face; they just made it so anyone who looked at me saw a dark void. I suppose I'm still a handsome devil," he joked. "All of us guards look alike and wear black and have no visible face. The only thing that makes us different is we retain our natural voices."

"You and Nina resemble each other," Bryce said. "You have different coloring, like Luke and I, but there is a strong facial similarity."

"I was thinking the same thing," Luke agreed.

"Me too," Amber said.

"That's because Nina is my long-lost sister. That was the next thing I planned to tell you," he said, smiling and turning to Nina. "You look a lot like our mother, except your eyes are the same color as our father's."

"*WHAT?*" Nina yelled at him, "How can that be?"

Laughing, David took her free hand in both of his, "I have an amazing story to tell you, little sister. But can we get something to eat? I'm starved, and haven't eaten in seven hundred years."

"You never ate in that place?" Nina asked.

"No. I was never hungry, no one ate anything," he replied still holding her hand. "The dimension's energy kept us alive without the need for food. I was, for all practical purposes, frozen in time."

"Why don't we send out for pizzas?" Amber asked.

"Will you make one of them a vegetarian?" Nina asked.

"Of course. That one will be for us and the guys can have the rest with all the meat."

"That sounds delicious," Luke replied and the others agreed with him.

"I'm on it," Bryce said leaving the room to call Valentino's.

David kissed Nina's hand before he let it go, saying, "Why do you think I saved your life and that of your beloved? I want to have a family again."

Nina knew he spoke the truth, and her heart was fluttering at this revelation. She had to admit that there was a strong facial resemblance between them. They had the same forehead, eyebrows, and eye shape. Their noses were different with his being more pronounced than hers and his jaw was square, where her face was oval shaped. Their smiles were identical.

"I am so grateful to you for saving our lives and surprised beyond belief that you are my brother. I have so many questions. I feel like I'm living a dream," she replied blinking back tears.

"A wonderful dream, and I'm eternally grateful," Luke said pulling Nina close to his side. "I hope that pizza gets here fast. I can't wait to hear the story."

"It will be about thirty minutes. Can I get anyone a drink? Or clothes?" Bryce announced.

"Another glass of water would be appreciated," David said.

"Beer and clothes," Luke requested.

"Beer for me too," Nina said.

"I'll go get them," Amber offered walking toward the kitchen, stopping to kiss Bryce on her way there.

"Why don't you all follow me upstairs and we can all get dressed?" Bryce asked noticing the dark, wet stains on David's cloak. "I have plenty of clothes to share."

"No, I actually enjoy standing around wrapped up in a blanket," Luke joked.

"I haven't worn real clothes in centuries, obviously," David said. "If it's not too much trouble, I would like real clothes too. I know I'm fairly tall and if you don't have anything, a clean robe will be fine."

"You're only two inches taller than I am. I'm sure I have some pants which will fit you. Luke may have to roll his up a bit," Bryce remarked.

"You only have three inches on me, bro," Luke replied. "Your pants might be a tad short on David."

"Follow me, gentlemen," Bryce said and they walked up the stairs. He was ecstatic that his brother and Nina were back and David was a hero.

"Amber, why don't you go get changed too?" Nina asked.

"I think I will. I don't want to be the only one standing around in a robe and my bare feet," she replied. "I'll be back shortly. Please make yourself at home."

Leaning her head back on the sofa, Nina closed her eyes. She couldn't believe her good fortune. With David's help, they rescued Luke and killed Elliott. She felt remorse for killing him, but that was the only way to put an end to his troublemaking and brutality. Seeing as everything happened while trapped in an alternate dimension, this was beyond any earthly court of law. She knew he would kill her and Luke when given the chance, and he almost did. Her thoughts wandered to Octo, and she hoped that without Elliott's energy giving it life, it would gradually weaken and vanish. Where the sword would end up was anyone's guess. Hearing heavy footsteps coming down the stairs, she turned her head and feasted her eyes upon three great looking men.

The guys were dressed in well-fitting jeans, slogan t-shirts, and sneakers. David had quite the body hiding underneath his robe. He possessed a lankier build than the Decker brothers, and his shoulders were broad and muscled, the jeans fit him to perfection. With his long hair, he reminded Nina of a rock star.

"What a handsome group of men!" she enthused.

"We all wear the same shoe size. You can call us the Bigfoot club," Luke jested.

Amber was next, descending the stairs wearing black jeans and a light blue, pullover sweater. She smiled seeing the three handsome men and remarked, "Nina and I are some lucky ladies."

Nina couldn't hold back her burning question any longer and asked David, "Did I live back in the past with you?" Her mind was working overtime trying to figure out the missing pieces of the past and how they lived in different centuries.

"No," David replied.

"Then how did you know I was your sister?" she asked.

"Once they made me a guard of the realm, my psychic abilities increased along with having superhuman strength. All I have to do is see someone and I instantly know their name and complete karmic history. It's like an instant software download to the brain. I'm familiar with the technology of your time. Aside from that, you look so much like Mother. She had dark hair and used to wear it down to her waist. She was petite like you. Father's eyes were the same color as yours, and your name was Risella. I was five years old when our parents were killed. The enchanted rock belonged to our Aunt Mori," he replied.

"Risella? That's kind of pretty. Tell me, big brother, where do we come from and why were you alive seven hundred years ago when I wasn't?" she enquired.

David took a sip of water and glanced around the room.

"Is everyone ready for this?"

"Yes. Tell us!" Nina urged.

"You and I come from another planet," he said.

Her mouth dropped open and the color drained from her face. She stared at him for a moment, too shocked to reply.

"I speak the truth. Our happy and peaceful planet was invaded by men carrying terrifying weapons and arriving in unusual aircraft. I watched them kill our parents from a secret hiding place. Then I ran as fast as I could to the nursery where Aunt Mori was watching you, and she said we had to leave. One of our elder wise women, Dani, operated the star gate, which is where we were going to escape to another planet. She programmed the star gate for planet Earth and we were supposed to land in America in this current century but something went wrong. Someone must have tampered with the controls because we entered the star gate holding onto each other's hands, and you were tucked safely in Mori's right arm, and we were separated, all of us. I could feel us being torn from each other and falling through a black abyss. I landed on the streets of 14th century London, alone. I was scared and crying. I didn't know what to do and wandered the streets for two days until a kind man named Edward Kellaway took me to his home. He and his wife didn't have any children and she had miscarried several times. He was a nobleman, a baron. They adopted me, changed my name to David, and raised me as their own. I told them my fantastic tale. I don't know if they believed it but it didn't matter. My adopted mother eventually had three children, all girls. They were wonderful people and I loved them, I always will. I grew up and became a knight and fought many battles until I was banished to the dark realm. So, there you have it," he said, with a sigh.

"Coming from another planet, how were you able to speak English?" Nina asked.

"I can't explain it, except that we were an advanced race of humans with the ability to talk to those who spoke a different language. I never questioned it. I don't know if you've experienced anything similar," he answered.

"Actually, I have," Nina said. "Many times when I hear people speaking another language, I know exactly what they're talking about. Do you think your psychic abilities from the dark realm will remain with you?"

"I don't know, but I hope so," he answered.

The sound of the doorbell made Amber jump and everyone burst out laughing. Bryce went to claim the pizzas and suggested eating in the dining room.

"It smells wonderful," David said. "I've never eaten pizza. I know what it is, but have never tasted it."

"You're going to love it," Amber said.

"It goes well with beer. Would you like one, David?" Bryce asked. "I imagine the beer you drank back in the 14th century was different than what we drink today."

"We called it ale. Yes, I'd like to try it," he responded.

"Give him a dark brew," Luke said.

"That's what I was thinking," Bryce said.

They settled at the table to eat, and David thought the pizza was heaven-sent.

"This is tasty. I want to eat pizza every night. And the ale isn't bad either."

Nina laughed, replying, "You'll get fat if you do that. What was the name of the planet we came from, and what was your name there?"

"My name was Tendaris. We didn't have last names. Our planet was called Arlom," he answered. "Our galaxy is far from Earth's and we have our own sun. I don't know what's become of it. I never knew what happened to Mori and Dani. I'm sure they ended up in another century like we did," he said. "What was your growing up like?"

"I was a ward of the state and grew up in different foster homes. My birth certificate lists a woman named Cindy Deveraux as my birth mother, and my father as unknown, but I knew that was a lie from the time I was small. I've always had psychic abilities and as I got older they increased and I learned how to astral travel. I wanted to find my birth mother, and the most I could see when I looked at my past was a young woman holding me and crying when she gave me up. I never saw my birth. I was supposedly born on February 8, which is the date listed on my birth certificate. My childhood was dreadful, and the foster families I stayed with just wanted me for the money the state provided them. I eventually fostered with a loving couple and their daughter, who was two years older than I. They adopted me, and I took their last name, Perotti. We are still close and I love them dearly, they saved my life. My sister's name is Madison. My life improved by leaps and bounds as I grew older, and I count my blessings every day," she said. "I think I must have landed on Cindy's porch, and she gave me an identity and a birthday."

"Our planet is like Earth and from what I remember, there were four distinct seasons in our region of Arlom. February isn't too far-fetched because I remember snow on the ground when you were born. And, our parents loved us," he replied. "There are many planets in other galaxies populated with humans. Some more advanced than others. The people of Arlom were quite advanced which is why things come easy to you."

"I'm glad you're here, David," she said, feeling at peace with finally knowing her true roots.

"Do you still have the ability to know everyone's karmic history?" Bryce asked.

"No. I remember some of yours from when we met on the astral. However, when I look at your lovely Amber, I'm not getting anything," he replied. "I hope that I can stay here in this century and finish what would have been my normal, earthly life. I was forty-three years old when I was sent to that realm. Back in those days, I was considered old. However, I was still in top physical shape and could fight better than the younger knights. My father, Edward, had recently died, and being his heir, I was the new baron. He outlived all his peers, and was a sharp old man until he died at the age of eighty."

"How does this dark realm work?" Luke asked.

"The realm is nothing but gray fog to those passing through on the astral. The dark karma which people experience when they arrive is a direct result of their karmic past. But there are exceptions to this. If someone has wished bad things for you, you will experience that in addition to the bad karma. The people and things you experience are creations from your own mind, and the antagonists or torturers are not real. They are like a vicious hologram come to life which disappears after they have done their harm or leveled the karmic playing field, and then you go onto the next punishment; most of the time. There are instances when adversaries will be there at the same time and torment each other, like what we just experienced with Elliott, Nina, and Luke. All of your past lives are recorded in the Akashic records for eternity, along with the karmic debts you have accumulated. Your current life is being recorded in the Akashic as well. That is why many astral travelers can view their past lives with all of the circumstances and people," he answered.

"Does someone have to be stabbed with the knife to get to this place?" Bryce asked.

"No. This realm or dimension has always existed. There are several ways someone can end up there, and not just with that knife or other spelled items," he replied.

"Like how?" Luke asked.

"People who abuse drugs and alcohol to the point where they hallucinate can find themselves trapped there. Practitioners of dark magic can use servitors to abduct their targets and bring them to the dark realm. People who commit suicide and fail to die have also landed there," he answered.

"How were you able to stand all those years of darkness, seeing people hurt and tortured every day?" Amber asked.

"By pretending it was just a play. I became numb watching the things people do to each other. A guard's main duty was to assist in keeping people alive for future torment until their predetermined time was up. People could commit suicide in this realm and many did rather than face their bad karma. Strangely, it doesn't feel like I was there for seven hundred years."

"Were we living parallel lives in different time periods?" Nina asked, trying to wrap her head around the time travel aspect of this situation.

"It would seem so. How could I have landed in the past, grew up, and at the age of forty-three was sent to another dimension for seven hundred years, and you landed in the current time, and have only been alive for thirty-eight years? It boggles my mind. I've heard it said there is no such thing as linear time and everything exists all at once," he said shaking his head. "I don't understand it, but I'm happy to be here."

"Your story is the most incredible thing I've ever heard," Amber stated. "I'm so thankful that you were able to save Luke and Nina, and yourself too."

"David, I think you should stay at my house," Nina stated.

"I was about to suggest that," Luke replied winking at her.

David melted at the kind offer his long-lost sister presented to him. He was deeply appreciative of being welcomed into not only her life, but Luke, Bryce, and Amber's too. The humble pleasure of enjoying a meal, good conversation, and laughter with friends and family made him feel alive again.

"I accept your offer, Nina. Although I'm from another place and time, I know much of your world's history and understand your technologies and current way of life. You live in an exciting time. I feel happy, and I haven't felt this way in *ages*," he laughed. "I would like to find a place of my own, eventually. I want it to be nearby so I can visit often. I'm hoping the rock will help me create enough money to live comfortably. I've learned that it works with an individual's energy field. I wanted to save you and Luke, and felt compelled to use it. I didn't know what I was doing, but it worked!"

"It does remarkable things," Nina said. "What is the story behind it?"

"Mori said that these rocks were abundant on our planet in ancient times, until a greedy king demanded they be mined for his use alone. Once the king's men mined every last one of them, they were kept in his private vault for a very long time until the palace caught fire and all of them were destroyed. Our great-grandfather had a few of these and gave one to Mori and our father, Dardon. She didn't know where father kept his hidden, but he carved the tree onto this one for her when she was a little girl. She gave it to me before we stepped into the star gate and when we became separated, I took it out of my pocket and accidentally dropped it. It fell through space and time. I know how you found it, and it makes me wonder if it was meant to find you and bring us back together. You put the original spell on that sword which Luke, or rather Magnus, made for you and you found it again too. Things have come full circle for us," he said.

"What? I made a sword and you spelled it?" Luke asked his eyes wide with surprise.

"I forgot to tell you! Once I stole the sword, I was able to view a past life where we lived in 13th century Scotland. You were a sword-smith named Magnus, and you made the sword for me shortly after we married. The laird of our clan, Callum MacNeal, had an affair with me before I met you, and he was mad that I cut him off after he got married. He wouldn't marry me because I wasn't a noblewoman, just the village healer. He came to see me when you were out hunting and tried to rape me. He didn't succeed, but he managed to steal the sword you made for me and kill you with it. He stabbed you in the back. Some friends of ours brought your dead body to me and I saw my sword stuck in your back. I was overcome with grief and anger. I pulled the sword from your back and put a spell of vengeance on it. Whoever owns the sword could stab their enemy with it and send them to a dark, hellish realm. In this realm, you would experience all the bad karma you ever did to another person, any dark wishes others wished on you would be fulfilled, and your deepest fears come to life until your earthly time was up. The spell obviously stuck, and that is how this whole thing began. It was all my fault, and I'm wondering how I knew of such a dark place back then," she explained. "I'm truly sorry for doing such a thing. I'm sure the spell has grown stronger over the centuries. I feel I should be punished for casting such a terrible, powerful hex. If we had the sword, I would attempt to break that spell. Oh, and Callum was Elliott. The man followed us into this life."

"David is right. Things have come full circle," Luke stated. "You might be able to break the spell on it without actually touching it."

"I've never cast a spell on an object in this life, but you're right. Maddie is the white witch in the family. I know she's done purification spells before that actually worked. Maybe the two of us will be powerful enough to dissolve it," she said.

"I think that is an excellent idea," David agreed. "Maybe the rock can help you with it."

"Then I'm going to get with her and we will make it happen," Nina said wanting to make it a reality as soon as possible.

"I have no doubt you will be successful. Even if it only weakens the existing spell, it will be worth it," Luke said. "Maybe I should learn metalcraft and start a side business called Magnus Metalsmithing."

"I've always wanted to try my hand at sculpting stone," David remarked.

"You guys should try those things. For the record, I would like to learn sword fighting," Nina said. "I'm hoping my big brother will teach me."

"It would be my pleasure," David replied.

"I was thinking ... maybe you can use the rock to find out what happened to Mori and Dani," Bryce suggested. "It would be interesting to find out what became of them. Perhaps they were sent far into our future."

"Something just occurred to me. I bet you could use that rock to conjure up a picture or a hologram of your parents and Mori," Luke said.

"That's a wonderful idea," David replied with raised eyebrows, looking at his sister. "Nina, would you like for me to try that?"

Touching his arm, she replied, "Yes, please do!"

The room became quiet as David closed his eyes, held the rock, and thought of their long-lost parents and aunt. In his mind's eye, he saw them as he last remembered, before their untimely deaths. He held onto the image until it materialized in front of everyone and continued holding it. He heard Nina inhale and knew he had been successful; he didn't dare open his eyes and break his concentration. He wanted her to have a good, long look at them. Her eyes filled with tears as she gazed at the hologram-like image of her biological parents. Her father was the same height as David, with golden brown eyes and light brown hair falling to his shoulders. He was wearing a green tunic, black pants, and sandals. Her mother was slender and petite with long dark hair cascading to her waist, and eyes of olive green, just like David's. She was wearing a long, cream-colored dress made of a silken material cinched at the waist with a rope belt. Her father had his arm around her mother's shoulders and she was holding Nina in her arms and smiling. Except for eyes of a different color, Nina was the image of her mother.

Mori's image was the last one to appear. She was tall, with long, light brown hair hanging half-way down her back and the same golden brown eyes as Nina and her father. She was wearing the same style of dress as Nina's mother, except it was dark blue. She had a sweet and pretty heart-shaped face.

"They're beautiful," she said with reverence. Reaching out to touch them, her hand went straight through. She couldn't hold back the tears and let them flow. Luke pulled her into his embrace and she cried against his chest. "All these years I thought my birth mother gave me up because she didn't want me. I kept searching for her, and now I know why I could never find her. I assumed my father deserted us or she never told him about me."

"You had no way of knowing, sweetheart," Luke replied. "You look just like your mother and David favors your father, but I can see both of them in both of you."

David felt his concentration faltering and took a mental snapshot of them. They vanished a few seconds later as a photo fell to the floor. He picked up the photo and was overcome with tears too, although he wiped them away quickly and forced himself to stop crying. There wasn't a dry eye in the house. Amber, Bryce, and Luke shed a few tears at the tender moment, remembering their own loving parents.

"Nina, I have something for you," David said.

She let go of Luke and turned toward David, "You took a picture!" she cried eagerly taking it from his hand. She hugged her brother and said, "Thank you. I'm so grateful to you. What were Mom and Dad's names?"

"Mother was Pinga, and Father was Dardon," he answered.

"That is amazing," Luke said.

"Yes, beyond incredible," Bryce commented, still mesmerized by what he had just witnessed.

"What about Dani?" Amber asked.

"I was so focused on our immediate family that I didn't think of her. Nina, would you like for me to conjure Dani?" he asked.

"Yes, I'd love to see her too," she replied.

David closed his eyes again and thought of the mysterious woman who managed the star gate. It was rumored that she was at least a thousand years old, descended from a master race of immortals. A few minutes later, they were looking at a woman of medium height who reminded Nina of a fairy godmother. Her thick mane of silken white hair hung down to the floor and her eyes were violet blue. She was quite pretty for an older woman and appeared to be in her early sixties. She was wearing a purple dress which complemented her eyes, and her smile was dazzling.

"Oh my God, she's lovely! She looks sweet, and a bit mischievous," Nina cheered.

David took a mental snapshot of Dani before her image disappeared. Like before, her photo fell to the floor and Nina retrieved it.

"I didn't have a lot of daily interaction with her, but she seemed like a kind lady and Mori thought the world of her," David replied. "Her name was Daneda and she liked to be called Dani."

"Did all of the women on Arlom have super long hair?" Nina asked.

"From what I can remember, yes. The clothing they wore was reminiscent of the 1960s hippie era. Quite a few people from that time accidentally found themselves in the dark realm due to the drugs they took," he responded.

"Can you astral travel?" Nina asked.

"Yes, I did so my entire life until landing in the dark dimension," David replied. "I'll try it tonight and see what I can find. I haven't truly slept in seven hundred years. In addition to not being hungry and living off of the energy, we didn't require much sleep either. We occasionally fell into a light sleep and suffered upsetting dreams of loved ones we left behind," he said.

"Well, it's time you started living again. Eating, sleeping, and having fun," Nina said.

Enjoying the warm camaraderie with his newfound family, David continued talking with them until the early evening.

"So, what are your plans for tonight?" Bryce asked them. "You're welcome to stay here if you want."

"Thanks, bro, but I want to go home," Luke said.

"How are you getting there? Are you going to teleport?" Bryce asked thinking this was the most unbelievable day of his life.

"Yes. It's the fastest way to get there," Nina said.

"Do you feel anything while you're teleporting?" Amber asked.

"No. It's as easy as snapping your fingers," Nina replied. "We must be physically connected to transport together. When you guys are ready we can join hands and head home."

"I'm ready. What about you David?" Luke asked.

"I'm ready too. Bryce, do you want your clothes and shoes back?" David asked.

"Not now. I can get them the next time we visit. We'll wash your robe for you," he said remembering it was lying on top of the clothes hamper in the bathroom.

"I don't want it back. Feel free to burn it," David stated.

Nina giggled, replying, "Good choice. You're starting a new life and don't need reminders of such darkness."

"Bryce and Amber, thank you for your kind hospitality. You've made me feel like part of the family," David said.

"That's because you are," Amber replied. "You are welcome here any time."

"Yes, and a million thank yous for saving their lives," Bryce added.

CHAPTER 8

Starting Over

Joining hands and using the enchanted rock, they teleported to Nina's house. "That's a great way to travel," Luke remarked. "No checking baggage, no connecting flights, no screaming kids kicking the back of your seat, and no airport security."

Nina laughed and said, "David, you and I are going to have to work out a timeshare for this rock."

"I think that can be arranged," he replied taking stock of Nina's house. "You have a nice home. It has a lot of space. Thank you for letting me stay here."

"You're welcome. The house is 2500 square feet and one level, so we won't be stumbling over each other. I'm still in shock that you are my long-lost brother, from another planet! I'm so happy you're here," she said hugging him.

"Me too, little sister," he replied, returning her embrace.

"Let us give you a tour of the house and tomorrow we'll show you the land. We have five acres, a horse, chickens, goats, a rooster, and no immediate neighbors to be concerned with," she beamed.

"Lead the way," David replied.

They gave him the grand tour, showed him his room, and he mentioned that he was hungry again.

"Why don't we take you out for dinner?" Nina suggested.

"That would be wonderful," David answered.

They chose the Chinese restaurant near Luke's new studio and David said he would have to resume sword practice and plenty of physical activity to maintain his physique, and then he could eat to his heart's content at the many delightful restaurants in this century. Luke told him he would be happy to be his training partner and they could learn from each other. Luke would teach him martial arts and David would teach him and Nina sword fighting. The three of them got along famously; one would have thought they had known each other for years instead of just one day.

After enjoying a hot shower, David relaxed on the comfortable bed with the intention of venturing to the astral to learn what happened to Mori and Dani. As a young boy, his adventures on the astral were exciting. He didn't know that he could use the astral to uncover hidden information until he was a grown man and accidentally found himself watching and listening to his enemies the night before a battle. Using this secret ability, again and again, he was rarely in a losing fight. He never thought about searching for his lost relatives this way until his discussion with Bryce. Welcoming the familiar sensations of body paralysis and some dizziness, he lifted to the astral. Looking down at his sleeping body, he thinks about flying and finds himself outside and soaring through the night sky. Reveling in his first out of body experience in centuries, he thinks of Mori and asks the universe to show him where she is. Nothing is shown to him and he abruptly falls from the sky and back into his bed.

Awakening with a start and fearing he'll never find out what happened to them, he vows to keep trying and becoming more proficient on the astral. He knew he was expecting too much from his first excursion. Tossing and turning for another hour, he reflected on the fantastic and fortunate events of the day until sleep claimed him again. This time he dreamt of someone he cherished. It was the same dream which haunted him repeatedly; one of several that he dreamt over and over in the dark realm. It never ceased to fill him with grief because he had never stopped loving her …

He was running his fingers through her long, silky hair shining in the sunlight. She gazed up at him with those captivating, azure blue eyes sparkling with joy.

"Cara, my sweet, seven more days and we shall be married. I can hardly wait to make you my wife," he professed and kissed her deeply.

"And just in time. It has been difficult hiding the morning sickness from my family," she replied.

"You know I would marry you even if you were not having my child," he said. "I wanted to marry you last year before I went off to fight."

"But I did not know you well, and there was talk that you were quite the ladies' man," she teased.

"Once I met you, all others ceased to exist," he responded. "There has been no one else but you since we first met."

She laughed and said, "I trust that will never change. We are lucky to have found a love match."

"There is only you, now and forever," he promised.

The next thing he knew he was down on both knees, crying un-abashedly at her grave. It did not matter to him that everyone watched him express his anguish. Suddenly bolting upright and turning to face his fellow mourners, he shouted, "WHICH ONE OF YOU MURDERED MY BETROTHED? YOU NOT ONLY KILLED HER, YOU KILLED MY UNBORN CHILD!"

He awoke wishing he had been poisoned too, dying along with her.

"One day I will have my revenge on you, Lily," he swore, thinking of the evil witch who destroyed their lives.

Late in the evening after David retired for the night, Luke and Nina lingered near the fire snuggled close together on the sofa. They were happy just holding each other and talking.

"I need to talk to you about something," he said.

"Is it David?" she asked.

"No," he replied.

Feeling apprehensive and turning to gaze into his eyes, she asked, "Okay. What is it?"

"How did Elliott know about the tattoo on your butt cheek?"

Smiling and laughing she answered, "Not in the way you think! I never had sex with him, or kissed him, or fooled around with him. He knows about my tattoo because we were at a party last year and we all got drunk. Several people stripped naked and jumped in the hot tub. They were trying to cajole the rest of us into joining them and I said no. I said that I didn't want everyone to see the butterfly tattoo on my right butt cheek and I didn't cavort in the nude. I probably shouldn't have announced it because it led to further teasing, but everyone had a good laugh and in my defense, I was pretty well lit. The skinny dippers in the hot tub started showing each other their tattoos and while they whooped it up the rest of us played blackjack. I came home with an extra seventy-five dollars. And that is the truth, so help me God."

"When Elliott was whipping me to shreds, he talked about how you fooled around with him, and that was how he knew about it. I hoped it was a lie, and even if it wasn't, whatever or whoever you did before we became a couple is irrelevant. I just wanted to know. I swear on a stack of bibles that you are and will always be the only woman I share my body with," he said kissing her sweetly. He had something else to ask her and was feeling uncharacteristically nervous, not to mention it was practically burning a hole in the pocket of his flannel shirt.

He got up from the sofa, stood in front of her, took her hands in both of his and said, "After everything we've been through, I have this overwhelming desire to make you my wife as soon as possible." Her heart was racing and she was at a loss for words. He bent down on one knee, reached into his shirt pocket and presented a diamond ring to her, "I know we haven't been together very long, but I know in my heart and soul that you are the one. I solemnly declare that I will love and treasure you for the rest of my life. For me, there is only you. Nina, will you marry me?"

She stared at the ring in shock. It was the same ring which had disappeared from the wooden box when Luke went missing. "Yes!" she exclaimed, and he slid the ring onto her left hand. He helped her off the sofa and hugged her close. "How did you get the ring from the box?" she asked.

"It was the craziest thing. When we were driving home tonight, I felt a light burning sensation on my chest, where my shirt pocket is. It wasn't hurting me; it was like my skin was very warm in just that area. While you and David were talking about horses, I went into the kitchen and found the ring in my pocket. I knew it was a sign from the universe. And I want you to know that I was planning to propose as soon as I could get to the jewelers and buy you a ring. I wanted it to be a surprise, and not have to ask you to pull the wooden box from its hiding place. This has been on my mind all day, ever since David saved our lives. How do you feel about getting married on Valentine's Day next month?"

"Yes! Yes! Yes!" she squealed and he hugged her tighter, spinning her around. They sealed their engagement with a passionate kiss.

"I'm so happy, I don't know what to do!" she squeaked.

"Let's go into the bedroom and make love," he said.

"All night long?" she asked.

"Till the rooster crows," he grinned. Picking her up and carrying her into their bedroom they made love until Rogue welcomed the morning.

⬥

David was drinking coffee when Nina and Luke joined him in the kitchen.

"It's about time you two got up," he kidded.

"Did you sleep okay last night?" she asked yawning.

"Yes. The bed was heavenly. I went to the astral but couldn't find Mori and Dani. I need more practice, and I'm going to keep working on it."

"Try using the rock next time," Nina said. "Hold it in your hand while you lift out."

"So, what do you think of coffee?" Luke asked pouring cups for himself and Nina.

"I love it," he answered, taking another sip. "I don't want to be a killjoy first thing in the morning, but there's something which is bothering me."

"What is it?" Nina asked.

"The sword. I think we should try to find it. It troubles me that a servitor has it. I know they need energy from their creator to remain potent, but who knows what strange or radical entity will take possession of it once Octo is gone. The possibility which concerns me the most is that Octo will find another source of energy to remain alive. What if he tracks us down here?"

"I've neutralized servitors before, but only on the astral," she said.

"Will you go looking for him?" David asked.

"Yes. I'll cloak myself so he doesn't recognize me," she responded. "I'm not sure, but I would be very surprised if he stabbed my astral body and I went back to the dark realm. I don't think it works that way. Don't worry though. I'll investigate while cloaked and let you know what I find. On a separate note, I'm happy to announce that Luke and I are engaged."

"Congratulations! I didn't think people got married anymore in this modern time," David said grinning. "When is the wedding?"

"Valentine's Day!" Nina cheered radiant with happiness.

"A lot of people don't take the plunge; however, there are still many who do. It's no longer a requirement. It depends on what the couple wants. There are a lot of people who marry, then get divorced, then remarry again and again. That *will not* happen with us. I know all couples say this going into a marriage, but I know without a doubt we will remain together," Luke declared reaching over and holding Nina's hand. "I'll do whatever it takes to keep her."

"And I'll do the same," she replied kissing his cheek.

"Are you planning on having children?" David asked.

"If it happens that would be great. But if it doesn't, we will still be happy," Nina replied.

"Same here," Luke said.

"David, I've been meaning to ask, can you move objects with your mind?" she was curious.

"Yes. It's a wonderful ability which we share," he replied. "I remember everyone could do that back on our planet. I had to be extremely careful growing up in England. People were superstitious and anyone suspected of being a witch was put to death. My parents knew of my special talent and kept my secret. Not even my sisters knew."

"You were lucky," Nina commented.

"I was. And now my luck has returned," he said smiling.

"I'll go hunting for Octo tonight and report back tomorrow morning," she said.

"Be careful," Luke and David said in unison.

"I promise I will," she replied. "David, we are going to adopt

Elliott's horse. His name is Morgan and I saw him last night, from the astral. He's doing fine but his food supply is low and he's been cooped up in his stable. We're planning to leave after breakfast to go get him. Do you want to come along?"

"I'd love to. And now that the sun is up I want to meet your farm family," he said.

"I'll make us a quick breakfast and then we can go," she said.

Cloaking herself as a black cat with yellow eyes and generating a protective field around her astral body, Nina ventured to the astral in search of Octo and the sword. She had a suspicion that Octo was no longer viable since his energy source had died. She viewed past events to determine his status and was pleased to watch him dissolve into nothing and the sword drop from his arm. No sooner had he dropped it than a woman with long dark hair wearing a colorful Mardi Gras mask swooped in and grabbed it. Nina's first thought was to track her down and steal the sword once more, and then she remembered Luke and David's pleas to be careful. She didn't want to jeopardize herself and risk the chance of ending up back in the dark dimension with no one there to save her. She had to know more about the person who took it. Frustrated by the turn of events, she slid back into her body. Staring at the ceiling, her mind was racing with ideas of how to get it back. Luke woke up and pulled her close.

"I'm guessing from the look on your face it's not going to be easy," he said running his fingers through her hair.

"Octo dissolved when Elliott died, and when he dropped the sword someone else swooped in and took it. I wanted to go searching for her but exercised caution instead," she sighed.

"I'm glad you did. At least we know Octo is gone and no longer a threat. He's not going to pop-in and stab one of us with it. Maybe we should let it go," he suggested. "After all, we don't know the woman who took it."

"I think you're right. Do you know that you soothe my soul?" she asked.

"I do now," he replied and kissed her.

The next morning they told David what happened and he thought it best to let it go too. His worry over a crazy servitor returning to cause them trouble was now a non-issue. As long as the person who took it never darkened their door, he could rest easy. Nina called Maddie and spoke with her at length about performing a purification spell on the sword. She thought it was possible and said she would arrive two days before the wedding and the two of them would work their magic.

David was adjusting to 21st century life as if he was born into it. He stayed with Nina for two weeks until moving into Elliott's former house. David worked magic with the rock, and things fell into place. He bought Elliott's home and Morgan came with it. Nina had taken Morgan into her care shortly after they arrived home, and David immediately bonded with the horse. His days were filled with learning new things. He learned to drive and bought himself a truck and a car. He learned to use a cell phone, computer, email, and every modern convenience available. He cut his hair and bought new clothes. He saw Luke and Nina often, because they had developed training plans for learning sword fighting and martial arts. Luke introduced David to Noah and they became fast friends.

Nina delighted in teasing Noah about marrying her sister, and when she showed him a picture of Maddie, he was anxious to meet her.

"She's pretty. You have my permission to set us up," Noah said admiring Maddie's smile, perfect teeth, long brown hair and deep blue eyes. "How old is she?"

"She turns forty in April," Nina replied.

"She looks ten years younger," he remarked.

Nina noted that David had a peculiar expression on his face when he saw Maddie's photograph.

"She looks like someone I used to know," he said drumming his fingers on the table and attempting to still his racing heart.

"Is that good or bad?" Noah asked knowing David's story and feeling he was a kindred spirit.

"Neither," David replied, shrugging his shoulders and changing the subject, "Hey, do you want to go target shooting next Sunday morning?"

"Sure. Nina, is Luke allowed to come along with us?" Noah asked grinning.

"I'm right here," Luke replied snickering. "But you've got the right idea. You'll have to count me out because we have a cake tasting at eleven on Sunday."

David's quick change of subject wasn't lost on Nina. She suspected something painful from his past which he wasn't ready to divulge, and she wasn't going to pry.

It was a busy, delightful, and joyous time for everyone, and Nina was thrilled that Luke wanted an active part in planning their wedding. Bryce and Luke had explored the possibility of having a double wedding, except that Nina and Amber had different ideas and each wanted their own special day. The excitement of Luke and Nina's upcoming nuptials inspired Bryce and Amber to set their wedding date for May 22.

Happy that her sister was safe and settled, Maddie accepted a temporary job in Patagonia photographing nature and animals. She promised Nina that she would be back in time for the wedding, and the purification spell, and asked her to order two sizes of the bridesmaid dress and she would wear the one which fit the best and return the other. This would be Maddie's last trip. She was financially secure, tired of traveling, and wanted to move closer to Nina. She was ready for a monumental life change. She offered to take the wedding pictures, but Nina wanted her to be in them, and hired another photographer instead.

CHAPTER 9

All for Love

As Luke promised Nina back in November, he refused a bachelor party and wanted to see his bride before the wedding. He had been a bachelor his whole life, and wasn't going to miss it. He would spend the night with Nina and bid her goodbye in the morning. They decided they would arrive separately at the church. He chose Bryce for his best man, and David to be a groomsman. He wanted Noah to be a groomsman too, but Nina wanted just two attendants. Noah happily agreed to be an usher along with Zac Phillips, a close family friend. Nina chose Maddie as her maid of honor, and Amber as a bridesmaid. The wedding would be small; they were expecting seventy-five people. Many of the guests were friends of Nina's from the rural co-op. Among those was a Unitarian minister who was delighted to perform the ceremony for them at his church. The reception would be held in a ballroom of the Hilton Hotel where their family members would be staying. Luke and Nina were spending their wedding night at an Embassy Suites close to the airport, since they were leaving for their Caribbean honeymoon the following morning. They decided against using the rock to teleport them to their romantic destination, preferring to experience the honeymoon journey with first-class plane tickets instead.

The wedding party and immediate family members were invited to the rehearsal dinner at an expensive and highly recommended seafood restaurant. Disappointed with her sister being a no-show for the rehearsal and dinner, Nina endeavored not to let it ruin this blissful time in her life. It wasn't Maddie's fault that a raging snowstorm in Dayton, Ohio, delayed her flight until tonight; and she was thankful that she abided by Maddie's wishes and purchased two gowns in different sizes. She prayed nothing else would go wrong. They would work on the purification spell as soon as Nina and Luke returned from their honeymoon.

"Don't fret so much, sweetheart. It's not like she's going to miss the wedding," Luke said placing his arm around her shoulders.

"I know, it's just that I really wanted her to be here," Nina sighed. "I haven't seen her in months, and hope she hasn't gained weight. What if neither gown fits?"

Luke burst out laughing and said, "I never thought my sweet little tomboy would turn into Bridezilla!"

His comment brought a smile to her face and she laughed. "You're right! I need to chill. She's on her way, we'll stay up too late talking, and everything will turn out fine. If neither dress fits, I will use the magic rock to fix it."

"Is she still planning to stay at your house while you honeymoon in Jamaica?" Noah asked.

"Yes," Nina answered. "And she'll stay for another two or three days after we get back."

"That's a prime opportunity for me to get to know her and show her around. She might fall madly in love with me and never return home," Noah joked.

"Keep dreaming," David teased, hiding his anticipation of meeting Maddie to see how much she resembled his dead fiancée in person.

As much as Noah was looking forward to meeting Maddie and hoping for a love connection, he couldn't stop thinking of a different woman. She had been heavy on his mind this past week. In his nightly astral adventures of helping lost souls find the light, one kept calling out to him and he couldn't find her. He knew that she was still attached to her physical body and not looking to go into the light. Her astral body found his and he felt a powerful attraction to her. She was tall, with long, light brown hair and eyes the same color as Nina's. He recalled the pictures David showed him of his long-lost family, and this woman looked exactly like his Aunt Mori. Although, he was having difficulty with the fact that she looked so young. If David's aunt was in her late twenties or early thirties when they went through the star gate, wouldn't she be a much older if not elderly woman by now? That alone made him question whether it was really her … *Unless she was being held captive somewhere like David and the aging process frozen in time.* He hadn't told anyone because he wanted to be positive it was her before he told David and got his hopes up. Her cry for help was stuck in his mind, playing in an endless loop … *"Help me, please! I need to escape before they kill me. I don't have much longer and I don't want to die."* When he asked her name and tried to follow, she vanished. It was the same scenario each night and he was genuinely concerned for her. David was still having problems with his astral travels and inadvertently finding dimensions where folks were partying and having a grand time and he relished participating in the fun every night. Noah, Luke, and Nina thought it was because deep down he just wanted to enjoy life again after spending so much time in the dark realm.

There was nothing Maddie hated worse than sitting on the tarmac going nowhere. She was anxious to get to Virginia for Nina's wedding tomorrow. She would have departed yesterday if a heavy snowstorm hadn't canceled all incoming and outgoing flights. It was now early evening, 6:30 p.m. Her flight was delayed one more hour and should take off at 7:30. This would have her arriving by 10:00. Nina and Luke offered to pick her up at the airport, but Maddie said she would take a cab to their house instead. She didn't want to inconvenience them at such a late hour. They offered to wait up for her. She was inwardly seething because she had already missed the wedding rehearsal and wouldn't make it in time for the rehearsal dinner at 7:00.

Not wanting to fuss with her hair, she braided the long, thick strands of chestnut brown into a French braid which trailed down to the middle of her back. She was a pretty woman even if she didn't consider herself as such. She was grateful that there was no snow in Charlottesville and the weather forecast predicted a balmy high of forty degrees with sunshine for the next several days. Bored with looking at pictures on her iPhone and growing increasingly restless, she gazed out of the window into the night reflecting on her life.

Divorced for three years, she recently changed her last name from Kramer back to Perotti, and swore she would never change it again for any man. She wouldn't even hyphenate it. Ryan Kramer was a fellow photographer who turned out to be a rotten husband. It was a happy marriage for the first two years and then he started lying, cheating, and in the last few months of their dying marriage, beat her up and put her in the hospital. He was dead now, killed in a car crash last year with some floozy he picked up at a bar. Despite her bad luck with men, she hoped Nina had finally found the one. At least she kicked Jerry to the curb when she caught him in bed with two women and called off their wedding. Maddie had given Ryan too many chances. She thought the world of Luke and had good feelings regarding her sister's upcoming wedding. Maddie was a true romantic at heart, and the excitement of meeting Noah Colton pulled her out of her gloom, even though she wouldn't meet him until the wedding tomorrow.

Nina said that he was six feet four with shoulder-length blond hair, which he wore pulled back in a ponytail. She said his face was ruggedly handsome with light blue eyes, dimples, and a scar which she didn't think marred his attractiveness. Maddie wasn't overly concerned with looks as long as he maintained good personal hygiene, good teeth, and a kind heart. She would probably date him because of his height alone. Being a tall woman at five feet nine inches, it was rare to find guys that much taller than she. She was excited to meet David as well. From the stories Nina told her, he sounded like a barrel of laughs.

Her plane departed earlier than expected at 7:00 and she breathed a sigh of relief. Finally able to relax, she closed her eyes and took a nap. She slept so soundly that she didn't feel the plane landing. She awoke with a start, realizing where she was. Walking off of the plane and giddy with anticipation, she made a beeline to the baggage claim area. She was so fixated on getting to her destination that she collided with another woman exiting the ladies room at breakneck speed, absorbed in her phone. The collision knocked both women backwards and onto the tiled floor. The woman's airborne phone crashed several feet away, breaking the screen. Maddie was the first to speak as they both stood up on wobbly legs.

"I'm so sorry! Are you okay?" Maddie asked, rushing over to the sullen woman who was staring back at her with evil eyes. She was dressed like a hooker, in black skintight leather pants, a white v-neck sweater that clung to her braless breasts, and stiletto-heeled boots.

"WHAT THE FUCK IS YOUR PROBLEM, BITCH?" the petite lady with the long dark hair and gray eyes screamed. *"I'M WEARING HEELS! I COULD HAVE BROKEN MY ANKLE!"* A few people were slowing down and staring, expecting a fight.

"I'm terribly sorry, but I think we're both okay. I'm on my way to my sister's wedding and I wasn't watching where I was going. You have my deepest apologies!" Maddie gushed with her hand over her heart which was pounding furiously.

A young boy walked over to the upset woman holding out his hand and said, "Excuse me, ma'am, is this your phone?"

"Yes, thank you," she replied, taking the phone and when she saw the broken touch screen huffed at Maddie: "You broke my phone!"

"Again, I am so, so, sorry. I'll replace it," she said reaching into her pocket for a business card. "Here's my contact information. Please call me and let me know how much it costs and I will send you the money."

The woman snatched Maddie's business card slipping it into her pants pocket. "You know, I could have been seriously injured because of you!" she shouted taking her tote bag and hitting Maddie over and over with it. Maddie tried to run and the woman grabbed hold of her backpack pulling her back.

"I'VE HAD ENOUGH OF YOU!" Maddie yelled, turning and punching the slutty woman so hard in the face that she stumbled backward again, this time into the arms of a man.

"Lily, honey, are you hurt?!" the handsome man dressed in a navy-blue suit asked as he caught her. She was breathless, staring at Maddie, who reminded her of someone she never stopped hating. In fact, she was a dead ringer.

"Yes. My face hurts. This Amazon bowled me over, broke my phone and punched me," Lily said with the best quivering voice she could manage and turned on the tears.

Two airport policemen came running over and one of them asked, "What's going on here? We had a report there was a fight."

"That's right, officer. This woman was rushing through the airport when she slammed into me and sent me to the floor. She broke my cell phone and when I tried to show her what she had done, she punched me in the face!" Lily cried.

"Is this true?" the officer asked Maddie.

"No! Well, part of it is. It's true we ran into each other, but we both landed on the floor. I didn't break her phone, it landed on the tile and the touch screen broke. I wasn't watching where I was going but neither was she! She had her head down, texting. I offered to pay for a replacement phone and gave her my business card and then she started hitting me with her giant tote bag. I tried to get away but she came after me, grabbing onto my backpack ... that's when I turned around and punched her. I know it was wrong, but she kept on hitting me with that bag and I had to make her stop. It was self-defense!" Maddie explained, riled up because something about this nasty woman made her want to pound her face into the floor repeatedly.

As luck would have it, there was no one left standing around to verify her story except for Lily's boyfriend.

"Can you tell me anything about this?" the other officer asked the man holding Lily.

"I can tell you that this woman punched Lily so hard that she fell backward and I caught her before she hit the ground," he answered.

"Did you see Lily chasing this woman and hitting her with the tote bag?" the officer asked.

"No. I turned the corner in time to catch her fall, though," the man said.

The officer turned to Lily and said, "Do you want to press charges?"

"Yes! I can feel my cheek starting to swell," Lily replied as blood seeped out the corner of her mouth. She purposely bit the inside of her cheek when Maddie struck her, and made herself slip and fall, knowing her man would be there to catch her and even if he wasn't, it was dramatic and made Maddie look like the bad guy. Maddie's punch had force behind it, and Lily used that to her advantage.

The policeman handcuffed Maddie while the other one read her Miranda rights and instructed Lily and her boyfriend to come to the police station and file charges. Maddie was in tears when they put her in the patrol car and took her away.

It was 11:30 p.m. and Maddie still hadn't shown up. Nina had called and left her two voice mail messages, and sent three unanswered texts. Luke checked arrival times online, and it showed that her plane landed promptly at 10 p.m. They both knew something was wrong, and Nina was about to go searching on the astral when her phone rang. She answered using the speakerphone so Luke could hear.

"Maddie?" Nina answered.

"I'm in jail!" she wailed.

"What?" Luke asked in shock.

"I got into a fight at the airport. I was running to the baggage claim and collided with an idiot woman who was face down in her phone. We fell to the floor, her phone broke and I apologized and offered to buy her a new one. Neither of us was hurt from the fall but she was fuming and hitting me over and over with her tote bag. I was trying to get away and she pulled on my backpack. I got sick of her shit so I turned around and punched her hard in the face. She fell backward and her boyfriend caught her. I know I shouldn't have done it, but she wouldn't leave me alone! The police showed up and she wanted to press charges. There were no witnesses except her boyfriend. No one saw her hitting me with the bag. Her face was swelling and the impact must have cut her mouth because I saw blood. Now I'm in the county jail. I'm so sorry Nina. I've ruined everything," she said sobbing.

"No, you haven't. Has the woman pressed charges yet?" Nina asked.

"No," she replied.

"I'm going to pay your bail and bring you home!" Nina declared.

"Maddie, that woman started this when she hit you with her bag. You had every right to defend yourself. I know some excellent lawyers. And I'm sure they can get the camera footage from airport security," Luke said.

"Luke's right. It wouldn't surprise me if she purposely ran into you. It was late and no one was around to dispute it. Believe me, we will take care of her," Nina soothed. "We're on our way right now."

"Thank you," Maddie replied still crying.

Nina paid Maddie's bail and the three of them drove home, arriving at 2 a.m.

"This is a terrible thing to have happened on the day of your wedding," Maddie sniffed.

"Let's get you settled and a nice hot shower. The wedding isn't until 12:30 and we have plenty of time. I have something which will help you sleep too," Nina said, trying to console her sister. "Or, if you want to talk, I'll stay up with you."

"I want to fall asleep and forget everything. Thank you both so much," Maddie replied. "I will pay back the bail money as soon as I can."

"You're welcome. And don't worry, everything will work out. Go wash away the day. And you'll feel better after a good night's sleep," Nina said.

She did just that, and the sleeping pill was a godsend. Luke and Nina were exhausted and sleep came quickly for them. Everyone slept later than usual, ignoring Rogue's morning greeting.

When Nina and Luke awakened, they had time for a lusty quickie before Bryce arrived at 7:45 to take him out to breakfast. The guys were treating Luke to breakfast, and then off to the church to get dressed and ready for the wedding. Nina walked with him to the door when Bryce showed up, and to her surprise David and Noah were standing on the porch with him, hoping to meet her sister. Amber was there too, with her bridesmaid dress in a garment bag and carrying a cosmetic case. She was going to cook breakfast for Nina and Maddie.

"Good morning," Luke greeted his friends.

"Good morning," they replied in unison.

"Noah and David want to meet Maddie," Amber announced.

"They will have to wait. She's still sleeping," Nina replied.

"That's right, she did get in late," Noah said.

"She ran into some trouble last night," Luke said with a grim face.

"What happened?" Amber asked.

"I'll let Nina tell you," Luke sighed.

"Did she start a fight?" David joked, and everyone snickered, except Luke and Nina.

"Come on guys, let's go eat and I'll explain everything. I'll see you at the altar, sweetheart," Luke said turning to Nina and kissing her.

"Stay out of trouble," she teased.

"You're all the trouble I want," he replied, and she watched the guys get into Bryce's vehicle, waving as they drove away.

"Are you hungry?" Amber asked.

"Yes, very," Nina said while Amber stepped inside, setting down her things in the sunroom on their way to the kitchen.

"Is Maddie okay?" Amber asked. "I noticed you didn't laugh when David was trying to be funny."

"I know he was just joking, but the truth is she *did* get into a fight at the airport, and the woman who instigated everything is going to press charges against her. Maddie punched her in self-defense. We bailed her out of the county jail shortly after midnight," she said.

"Seriously?" Amber asked in awe.

"Yes," Maddie said walking toward them wrapped up in a plush, royal blue robe and socks. Her long hair was in a messy braid.

Amber introduced herself and said with concern, "I'm sorry you had such a bad time last night."

"Oh, so am I. It's nice to meet you," Maddie replied with a small smile. She was an emotional wreck and trying to remain calm.

Nina gave her a big hug and said, "You don't have to keep it all bottled up. I know this is my wedding day, but if you need to vent, cry, or scream, I'm listening."

"Me too," Amber volunteered. "Would you like omelets for breakfast or pancakes or both?"

"I'd really like pancakes this morning. Is that alright with you, sis?" Maddie asked.

"Sure. I have blueberries too."

"That's even better," Maddie loved blueberry pancakes and Nina was happy she remembered to buy them.

"You two sit down and enjoy your coffee, I'll make the pancakes," Amber said.

"Is it okay if I borrow some underwear and toiletries? My suitcases are sitting in baggage claim and I won't be able to get them until sometime later tonight," Maddie asked.

"Of course. You can use or borrow anything you wish," Nina replied.

"What a woman!" David enthused when Luke finished telling them of Maddie's predicament. "Noah, are you man enough for her?"

Noah laughed replying, "Totally."

"Maddie's a sweet person. I hate what happened," Luke said. "I'll have my sources do an investigation on this Lily Nolan bitch."

David choked on his orange juice when he heard that name. Recovering quickly, he suffered a minor bout of coughing.

"Are you going to make it?" Bryce asked.

David gulped down a glass of water and answered, "I think so. Something went down the wrong pipe."

"Do you know her?" Noah asked.

"It was seven hundred years ago. It can't be the same Lily Nolan," he replied. *If it is, I want the pleasure of killing her. I'll set her on fire; that kills evil entities.* He didn't want to share the sad story that had taken the life of his sweetheart centuries before. This was supposed to be a happy day.

"Maybe she won't press charges," Bryce mused. "Even if she does, I think we have enough *magical powers* to make all of this disappear."

"Yeah, I've thought of that too," Luke agreed. "We won't let Maddie do time."

"I second that motion," David said.

"What if it is the same Lily? We all belong to the secret inner circle of *weird*," Noah commented.

"We'll find out soon," Luke promised. "I guess the upside is that it will be quite a story to tell our children and laugh about one day."

Lily was tickled that Maddie got thrown in jail. She was going to relish the next several days knowing the woman would be miserable and living in fear. She was excited to have the sword back, too. While applying her eye makeup, she entertained thoughts of stabbing Maddie with it. Adding to her wicked delight, she was getting close to the finish line with another bad guy. He was on his way to her hotel room for a rendezvous and she would take his essence today. She smiled thinking about what an asshole he was. She wasn't planning on having another man this soon until she laid eyes on him. He was more handsome than most, and a cutthroat businessman who rose to his current CEO position by lying and backstabbing. He cheated on his wife at every opportunity, and that turned Lily on even more. If she kept up her current streak of luck bedding bad guys, she might be able to take a long vacation soon. Looking out her hotel room window at the rolling hills, she couldn't stop thinking of the woman who punched her in the face. She would find her and make her pay.

Maddie was feeling considerably better after coffee and breakfast.

Amber's pancakes were the best she'd ever tasted. She appreciated that her sister and Amber were understanding and encouraged her to unburden her soul, which she did.

"We should start getting ready," Nina said looking at the clock. "I've had a great time this morning and the pancakes were awesome."

"I'm glad you liked them. Maddie, you seem a bit more cheery," Amber said.

"The sun is shining and weddings are happy occasions, especially this one," she replied.

"And two handsome men are anxious to meet you," Nina said.

"I better go make myself pretty," Maddie replied.

"Me too," Nina agreed. "I'm happy I bought a house with three bathrooms. We can make ourselves beautiful without stepping on each other's toes."

An hour and a half later they were transformed into beauty queens. Maddie was pleased that the smaller sized dress fit her perfectly. After being called an Amazon, she was feeling gawky, large, and self-conscious.

"You are so pretty, and tall and elegant," Amber said appraising the goddess in the mirror.

"Thank you, but I've always wanted to be petite like you and Nina," Maddie replied.

"No you don't! Stand up straight, arch your back and push those boobies out," Nina scolded, half-teasing. "You look fabulous, and if Noah doesn't fall at your feet, I know another man will. You should be thankful that you can reach things on the top shelf."

"Not always. I'm only five feet nine," Maddie replied, laughing. "And now that I'm putting on these shoes, make that five feet eleven."

"No worries. Noah is six feet four," Amber added.

"Okay sis, now it's your turn," Maddie said and they helped her into her gown.

"You are a vision of beauty!" Amber remarked while Nina

admired herself in the cheval mirror, turning this way and that to get a good look at each angle. She was wearing a semi-fitted, slightly A-line, white silk gown with a detachable, chapel-length train. The sweetheart neckline was off her shoulders and adorned with tiny seed pearls. On her head was a delicate crystal and pearl tiara with a red, heart-shaped crystal in the center. The attached sheer white veil ran the length of her dress in the back, and she opted to wear it off of her face instead of having Luke lift it during the ceremony. She wore a matching crystal and pearl necklace with a red heart in the center. Her short dark hair and recently acquired spray tan accentuated the color of her dress. She looked exquisite. Amber and Maddie wore matching dark red, floor length silk dresses in an off the shoulder style similar to Nina's dress. The color and the dress was flattering on both women.

"Luke will be awestruck when he sees you," Maddie said with a big smile. "How much do you want to bet that a tear rolls down his cheek when he says his vows?"

She giggled, replying, "How much did you have in mind?"

"Fifty dollars," Maddie announced with mischief in her eyes.

"So, if he doesn't cry, you owe me fifty dollars?" Nina clarified.

"Exactly. And if he does cry, you owe me fifty dollars," she agreed. "I know I'm going to win."

"I don't think he will cry. He's not the type," Nina professed. "I accept your bet!"

"I wouldn't be too sure about that," Amber cautioned good-humoredly. "Luke has surprised me more than once since he fell in love with you. I never knew he was such a romantic."

"I truly don't think he will cry, but I might," Nina replied. "The waterproof eye make-up was an excellent idea."

"I have a lot of experience with that. You'll be thanking me after the wedding," Amber joked.

The doorbell rang and Nina said excitedly, "The limo is here!"

"I'll let them know we are almost ready," Amber offered, making her way to the door.

"Are you taking his name?" Maddie asked.

"Yes. No hyphenation either. I like the sound of Nina Decker," she replied.

The ladies walked out the door a few minutes later and stepped into the long white limousine carrying Nina's detachable train in a garment bag.

"Was this Luke's idea?" Amber asked.

"Yes. And this is the same limo which will take us to the reception," she replied.

"I love happily ever after," Amber said.

"Me too," Maddie replied.

Nina's parents, Gabe and Claire Perotti, were waiting for them at the church. There was a separate building attached to the church for special events and the limo dropped Nina and her attendants off at an entrance where they wouldn't be seen by Luke. They just missed the florist who delivered the bridal bouquets, boutonnieres, and flower arrangements for the altar. Luke had been watching out for the flowers because he had a special note he wanted to place in Nina's bouquet. He breathed a sigh of relief when he intercepted the deliveryman and placed the little pink envelope in between several flowers of her bouquet. Her mother saw him do this and gave him a smile and nod of approval. She carried the bouquets to the dressing room.

Claire also wore a red dress. It was knee length with a swingy skirt and matching bolero jacket. In her early sixties, she was an attractive woman of medium height who looked much younger. She refused to let her hair go gray and kept it a pretty shade of dark auburn which enhanced her brown eyes.

"My darling girl, you are a lovely sight to behold," she said, walking over to hug Nina.

"Thanks, Mom," Nina replied.

"I'm so happy for you and Luke. You two have overcome so much in a short period of time, it's beyond belief. I know you will be happy together," Claire said. "Your father and I are delighted you've found David too. He's a fun-loving, remarkable man, and handsome too. We adored talking with him last night. There's no mistaking you two are related. I told him if he ever needed any motherly advice that he could call on me."

"If my flight hadn't been delayed, I could have met him with the rest of you last night," Maddie sighed, pondering the best time to tell her parents she was thrown in jail for assault and battery. She decided to wait until after Nina and Luke left for their honeymoon.

"Sweetie, you look fabulous," Claire stated, approving of how the dark red dress enhanced Maddie's pretty face and complemented her long chestnut hair.

"I'm glad you think so. Nina's trying to fix me up with Noah Colton," Maddie quipped.

"I think he would be perfect for you," Nina said. "I don't see how he could resist such a beautiful woman."

"I agree. He's a sweet, gentle giant and we enjoyed talking with him," Claire replied. "I want to see both of my girls happily settled down with a good man."

"The flowers are gorgeous!" Amber praised, picking up her bridesmaid bouquet. Their bouquets were red and white roses, smaller versions of Nina's bridal bouquet. "When Bryce and I get married, we'll have lots of roses too."

"Your big day is coming up soon and will be here before you know it," Nina replied, feeling full of love and happiness and looked at her bridal bouquet with a raised eyebrow. "Why is there a pink card in mine?"

"You'll have to open it and find out," Claire replied with a sly grin.

Maddie fought a surge of jealousy, wishing she could find love again before she got too old. As much as she was looking forward to meeting Noah, she had a feeling it wouldn't work out somehow. She picked up her bouquet, inhaled the sweet roses and tried not to think of the mess she made of her life by getting arrested last night. She steeled herself to wait until her fortieth birthday in April to ugly cry and wallow in self-pity.

Nina was about to open the pink note when she noticed the unhappiness on Maddie's face. She walked over to her sister knowing exactly how she felt.

"Don't worry. I know that you won't be convicted of anything, and you will find love again, I'm certain of it. The man in your sexy dreams will make himself known."

Maddie couldn't help giggling at her sister's comment. "I wish he'd hurry up!"

"Sometimes you find love where you never expect it," Amber said. "Nina, aren't you going to open that pink note?"

"Yes, right now," she replied, turning over the envelope and seeing that it was sealed with a golden rose sticker. Carefully opening it, she never expected anything like this,

To my lovely Nina,

I'd pull the stars down from the sky for you,
So that you would know my love is forever true.
I'd walk thousands of miles through desert sands,

Just to feel the touch of your loving hands.
No woman is more precious and adored, for me you are the one,
My love for you burns a million times brighter than the sun.

You hold my heart, my soul, my life,

And I will cherish the sweet moment when you become my wife.

Yours now and forever, Luke.

Nina was stunned and deeply touched. Taking a deep breath, she said, "I don't think I could love him more than I do right now."

Tears rolled down her cheeks and Maddie handed her a tissue, saying, "You're a very lucky woman. I hope the next time around I find a man at least half as good as Luke. Do you mind if we read it?"

"No, of course not," she replied handing it to Maddie as Amber and Claire moved closer to see what Luke had written.

"Wow." Amber took in a breath.

"Be still my beating heart. You hit the jackpot, little sis. He's a tough act to follow," Maddie commented with a half-smile.

"I'm so glad you didn't marry Jerry," Claire remarked.

"Me too," Nina said.

"Love rules the day," Amber declared just as Zac stepped through the door and said, "It's time!"

Maddie, Amber, and Claire filed out to begin the procession. Gabe remained behind with Nina.

"My dear, there are no words to describe how beautiful you are," he said drawing her into his embrace.

"Thanks, Dad," she replied, blinking back tears, still emotional from Luke's love poem. It was too early for crying and she had to make it through the ceremony. "And you look handsome in that tuxedo."

"I can't tell you how happy I am that you are marrying Luke and that you found your long-lost brother. They're both exceptional men. I believe you got it right this time," he said. "I know you are a strong and independent woman, however, I still worry about you and knowing there will be a worthy man to love and help keep you safe eases my mind considerably."

"My very own archangel Gabriel still looks after me," she replied, gently pulling away to look at the man who welcomed her into his family and shaped her early teenage years, taking away the hurt and pain of feeling alone and scared. Now in his late sixties, he was still robust with a full head of hair, albeit completely gray. His eyes were a darker shade of blue, like Maddie's.

"You were my first hero," she said wiping an errant tear from her face.

Laughing softly, he replied, "A father loves to hear those kinds of things. You know that your mother and I love you like our own flesh and blood."

Nina smiled and said, "Same here. Well, I guess you better walk me down the aisle now. If we stay here talking like this, I'll be crying buckets in no time."

He extended his arm to her, saying, "Let's go, princess."

"I never thought I'd see the day when you would get married before me, or at all," Bryce teased.

"Stranger things have happened … literally!" Luke laughed, fastening his bow tie. "You're not far behind bro, just three more months."

"Are you nervous?" Bryce asked.

"Not one bit. I'm one hundred percent sure about this," Luke replied. "What about you?"

"Are you kidding? I was the one in favor of having a double wedding today, but the ladies wanted their own special day, which I totally understand," Bryce replied. "Amber's always wanted a spring wedding."

"Yeah, I know. I have to say it is a coincidence that Valentine's Day falls on a Saturday this year. We couldn't have timed it better," Luke stated.

"I'm surprised that Nina wanted to go all out for your wedding," Bryce remarked.

"Despite her tomboy tendencies she's a romantic girly girl deep down," Luke replied. "She even likes glitter toenail polish, and her favorite color is pink. Sometimes I paint her nails."

David roared with laughter, asking, "Is it a prelude to something kinky?"

Bryce laughed along with him and Luke replied, "I'm secure enough in my manhood to admit I enjoy painting her nails and yes, it often leads to other things which I won't share with you two."

Seeing that the door was open, Noah walked into the room and announced, "It's time. Get your butt to the altar, Decker."

"Now I get to meet Nina's sister. Is she as pretty as her picture?" David asked.

"We'll find out shortly," Noah replied.

"She's very pretty, although not gorgeous like Nina," Luke answered and they filed out of the room.

"Yep, he's in love," Noah stated.

The men were gathered in the hallway waiting for the mother of the bride, maid of honor, and bridesmaid. A string quartet was playing classical Baroque music, filling the church with a light and cheerful ambience.

Noah and David were in awe when they laid eyes on Maddie, watching her long and shapely form walking toward them. Noah smiled and winked at her and then took Claire by the arm to escort her down the aisle to her seat. He thought Maddie was beautiful, and eagerly anticipated the reception when he would get to talk with her. Seeing her in person made him forget about his astral crush, and he told himself he should pay more attention to flesh and blood women. David was smitten at first sight, deciding in a split second that Noah wasn't going to have a chance with her.

Maddie thought Noah was attractive, tall and rugged looking, and she didn't mind his scar; she thought it added character. As her sister said, his blond hair fell to his shoulders and he wore it pulled back in a ponytail. She normally didn't like that look on a man, but it looked great on him. His blue eyes were warm and kind. However, when her eyes locked with David's her heart was pounding … *My God, he's handsome!* The two of them stood speechless, staring at each other until Bryce nudged him.

"Maddie, this tongue-tied man is David," he said, stifling the urge to laugh.

"It's nice to meet you, David," she said … *Déjà vu, somehow I know you.*

"You're the most beautiful woman I've ever seen," David replied taking her hand and bringing it to his lips, his eyes never leaving hers.

"Thank you," she replied, allowing him to take her arm and they walked down the aisle. He was proud to be escorting her and they made a beautiful couple. Maddie liked the fact that she could look up to a man for a change. In her mind, she thought every man should be six feet four or taller. Noah was perceptive, and when he saw the two of them walking the aisle together, he knew David would be putting the moves on her before the reception. He was stung with jealousy for a brief moment but it passed, and he thought for some unknown reason that Maddie and David belonged together.

"I don't think Noah stands a chance," Amber whispered to Bryce.

"You're right, he doesn't," he replied. "How much do you want to bet they'll be doing the horizontal mambo tonight?"

Amber giggled and replied, "I'm not betting with you. You always win!"

He kissed her cheek and said, "I do, and you are my grand prize."

After Bryce and Amber walked the aisle and took their respective sides at the altar, the bridal march began playing and Gabe and Nina proceeded down the aisle. Even though Maddie and David were watching them make their way to the altar, they cast several discreet glances at each other. She knew she wouldn't be dating Noah.

Nina's eyes locked with Luke's, and the sight of her stole his breath away. He said a silent prayer thanking God over and over for the miracle that was Nina. She had never seen him in a tuxedo, and he was a sight for sore eyes. She thought he looked so fine in his fitted black tails, the jacket enhancing his wide shoulders and narrow waist. She said her own little prayer, thanking the universe for the remarkable man she was marrying today.

Gabe kissed her cheek and she joined hands with Luke. The minister welcomed the guests, said a prayer and blessed the wedding rings. They had written their own vows, and Luke was the first to speak.

"Nina, my love, thank you for being my best friend, my fantasy, and my wonderful reality. You are the great love of my life, and I promise to love, honor, cherish, and be faithful to you. I promise to be there whenever you need me, to be your protector and your safe haven. I adore you. I am honored that you will have me for your husband. I pledge myself to you for eternity," he said slipping a gold ring on her finger.

"Luke, I am overjoyed to become your wife, and I promise to love, honor, and cherish you for the rest of my days and beyond. You are the great love of my life and you make me the happiest woman in the world. I vow to be faithful to you and always be there for you. I am yours forever and a day," she stated sliding a band of titanium steel on his finger. She saw the tears escaping from his eyes and smiled as her own started to fall.

The minister spoke about love and commitment before saying, "I now pronounce you husband and wife." Luke pulled Nina to him and kissed her. "And yes, now you may kiss the bride," the minister said laughing and the guests erupted in applause.

Luke and Nina finally broke their kiss and he lifted her into the air. He wanted to twirl her around but was afraid they would get tangled up in her train. Instead, he lowered her to the floor and whispered in her ear, "You're the best thing that ever happened to me."

"I love you, Luke," she whispered back, kissing his cheek. "And the poem was beautiful."

The happy couple turned around, clasped hands, and walked back down the aisle smiling and glowing with happiness. Amber and Bryce followed behind them, holding hands and thinking about their upcoming wedding.

"That will be us in three months. Still want to take the plunge?" he asked, smiling.

"You know I do. What about you?" she teased back.

"Absolutely," he replied.

David took hold of Maddie's hand and they followed after Bryce and Amber. He couldn't help himself and entwined his fingers with hers. She could feel her face turning red and loving the feel of his strong hand; it felt so right, like they had done this before. The attraction between them was intense. Her thoughts wandered to the sexy dreams she'd been having lately, and she hoped he would make them come true tonight. He wanted to take her back to his house and up to his bedroom and keep her there permanently. The plan was to join Bryce and Amber in the lobby and mingle while Nina and Luke received congratulations from their guests. Instead, he led her to the room where the men had gathered to get dressed for the wedding. Once inside he stopped, turned to face her, and took her pretty face in his hands.

She couldn't look away from his adoring gaze, and before she had a moment to speak, he kissed her. She returned his kiss, opening her mouth for a deeper experience. When their lips parted he embraced her, holding her close, and whispering in her ear, "Cara, my love. I never thought I would see you again."

Until next time...

Also By Laura Simmons

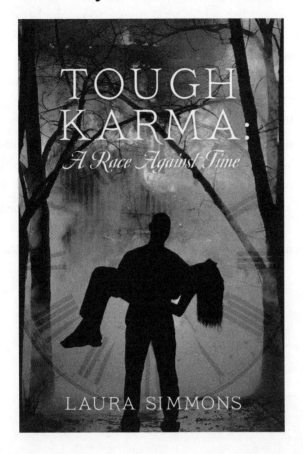

Tough Karma: A Race Against Time

Amber Macklin's world is cruelly shattered when she loses her baby girl three months after her husband's sudden death. Her cousin, Bryce, comes to her rescue, moving her into his home for fear she will kill herself from the grief. He provides solace and a shoulder to cry on, and he has loved her as more than a cousin for a long time. Amber and Bryce soon discover they are not blood relatives, which opens the door for romance as he pulls her through her darkest hours.

When Mike, a college friend of Bryce's, stops by to visit, Amber senses a deadly secret behind his nice guy persona. She has a frightening dream that Mike is trying to kill her and recurring sleepwalking episodes where she draws detailed pictures of him torturing her. Deeply troubled, Bryce uses his ability to astral travel to investigate Mike and uncover his terrifying past.

Mike has had his eye on Amber for some time, and when he learns that Bryce and Amber have become lovers, he is furious. Mike abducts Amber and takes her to his rural Georgia hideaway, and Bryce must rely on his astral abilities to track her down. But will he be too late?

Learn more at: www.outskirtspress.com/toughkarma

CPSIA information can be obtained
at www.ICGtesting.com
Printed in the USA
BVHW030247151121
621678BV00004B/259

9 781977 201553